191084

This book is to be returned on or before
the last date stamped below.

Someone Came Knocking

Someone Came Knocking

Anne Merrick

Spindlewood

For Brian
and all our children and grandchildren.
With love.

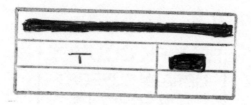

First published in Great Britain in 1993 by
Spindlewood, 70 Lynhurst Avenue,
Barnstaple Devon EX31 2HY

Copyright © Anne Merrick 1993

British Library Cataloguing-in-Publication Data.
A catalogue record for this book is
available from the British Library.

ISBN 0-907349-32-3

Typeset by Chris Fayers, Soldon Devon EX22 7PF
**Printed and bound in Great Britain by
Short Run Press Ltd., Exeter**

PART I

Mort

Chapter 1

As he toiled up the street from the river Tod could feel the big stone in his chest where his heart ought to be. It was heavy and hard and cold and it weighed him down.

Pushing his hands into the pockets of the old duffle coat which draggled almost to his ankles, he scowled into the early darkness. Fog rising from the river seemed to press gently at his back and all around him it was filling the hollows between the buildings, smothering the street lights, extinguishing the last gleam of the day. Half-way up Old Bridge Street he sidled into the doorway of a boarded-up shop and stood hunched against the wall watching the flow of people and traffic on the hill. It was nearly closing time and everyone was going home. Soon the streets in this half-demolished quarter of the city would be quiet and he would be able to set about Mort's fishing. He yawned and as he drew in a deep breath of damp air there came with it the smell of something frying from the dingy Indian take-away on the corner. Tod's mouth watered. He hadn't eaten for hours. But he knew from experience that The Paradise Garden was secure against begging, borrowing or stealing. Perhaps he should try the Market Hall. With any luck, the stall-holders would be too busy tidying up to notice him.

Leaving his doorway and keeping close to the walls, he went on up the hill past the blacked-out window of the shoe repairers, the gaudy lights of the amusement arcade, the Witches and Halloween masks of the joke shop.

As he turned into the side street which led to the back entrance of the Market, he was caught in the glare of neon lighting from the windows of a big store. A boy of indefinite age, his slight frame swamped by the overlarge coat, his pale face darkened by grime. And beneath a tangled ash-coloured fringe, eyes that were as grey and lightless as the fog. Shrinking from the light, pulling his hood over his head, he scurried on into the safety of the shadows.

Opposite the Market a skip was standing among the rubble of what until last week had been a terrace of three houses. From long practice Tod noted it but it was too soon to start fishing, too many people still about, and he crossed the road with barely a glance at it. A flight of steps led straight from the pavement to the swing doors of the Market Hall. A scum of paper wrappers, plastic bags, and stumps of rotting vegetables lined the gutter and washed up against the lowest step. Tod's eyes scanned it briefly for anything that might be useful or eatable before he began to climb.

He was about half-way up when from behind him he heard yelps of laughter and a heavy trundling sound as if a sledge were being dragged over the debris of the building site. Startled he looked round and saw two boys tugging on a ramshackle, home-made trolley whose metal wheels had snagged on a heap of broken bricks.

The boys were larking about, laughing too much to put enough effort into freeing the cart which was weighted down by another boy who lay slumped against its raised back. Curious for a moment Tod stood and watched as the taller of the two boys ran round to the back of the trolley and leaning against it pushed it hard. The wheels rattled suddenly free, jolting the cart so that the boy sitting on it was thrown forward. He didn't move but lay as he had fallen, folded double, head lolling over his feet. The smaller boy shrieked again with laughter and, instead of helping him up, aimed a powerful kick at his sagging shoulders. Tod winced as the figure on the trolley rolled slowly sideways, toppled off the wooden seat and sprawled face down among the bricks.

Coughing in the fog which was thickening like smoke around them, the two boys hauled him up and propped him once more on the cart. During all this he made no movement of his own. Against his usual inclination to steer clear of other children, Tod found himself leaving the Market Hall steps and moving towards the boys. But absorbed in what they were doing they did not notice him until his feet crunched on the scree of the building site. Then looking up they saw, dim as a dream through the fog, only the long dark folds of his duffle coat and under its hood a face as white as bone.

"Gawd!" said the taller one, "What's that?"

The other one giggled uneasily, "Looks like a ghostie!" he muttered.

Tod stood still and pointed to the trolley, "What's the matter with him?" he asked. "Why doesn't he move?" His voice, so little used, came out scarcely above a whisper.

Both boys stared at him, the expressions on their faces changing from uncertainty to jeering disbelief.

"Prob'ly cause 'e died!" said the smaller one, "a couple 'undred years ago!" Then pulling at his friend's sleeve, he said, "C'mon. Move it! This ghostie stinks! Stinks worse 'an a dead fish!" and pinching his nose between finger and thumb he moved back to the cart. The other boy hesitated and as the gap between them widened and the fog momentarily swirled away from them, Tod saw clearly for the first time what lay on the trolley.

It was not a boy at all. It was merely a set of clothes stuffed and padded out to look like a boy. It was a rag-doll, a scarecrow, a guy. An old tweed jacket held together its body of straw and at its neck a fringed silk scarf was tied in a scarlet bow. Under a woollen hat its sackcloth face was garishly painted, the eyes stony white, the mouth a red gash beneath a curling black moustache. As it stared sightlessly into the fog there was something raffish about its expression. Something almost appealing.

The boys yanked hard on the tow-rope, the trolley bumped over the bricks and the guy's head jerked and nodded.

"He looks as though he's talking," said Tod.

"Yeh!" said the little one. "Dessay 'e's askin' yer fer a penny!'

"Gerroff," said the other, "Askin' 'im! 'E looks more like a guy than the guy do!" And steering a wide berth around him they moved off along the road.

Tod snarled. Bending down he snatched up a handful of stones and shards of brick and flung them at the boys' retreating backs. Laughing they broke into a run and the fog drew them into itself. As he dragged his feet back towards the Market steps Tod could hear them calling in the distance. "Penny for the Guy, Mister? Penny for the Guy?" He should have known of course — from the display in the joke shop window — Halloween now, Bonfire Night soon.

"Here am I... a poor old Guy... legs in the bonfire... head in the sky..."

The words floated into Tod's head from nowhere. Or rather they came from a place somewhere deep inside him, a place which ached when he tried to reach it, like a painful tooth probed by a tongue. But as he pushed through the swing doors of the Market Hall and scuttled for the nearest cover, more words put themselves together in his head.

"Ay, all I am made of... only trash is... And soon... soon... Will be dust and ashes."

The stone in his chest swelled against his ribs. Seeing a book which had fallen from a stall, he pressed his foot upon the open pages, smearing and tearing them as he ground them down into the dust.

Wedged between two derelict neighbours, Mortimer's Junk Shop stood at the lower end of Old Bridge Street where the hill flattened out towards the river. By the time Tod returned there he was sweating with pain. The Market Hall had yielded only a withered apple and a gristly rasher of raw bacon and his stomach was now griping either with hunger or the effects of eating bad food.

The roll of carpet he'd fished out of a back yard in Sebastien Street kept slipping off his shoulder and hoisting it back he squinted through the window. At the back of the shop a standard lamp, its red shade askew, cast a sleazy light over the clutter of things which filled the space; ironing boards rubbed shoulders with lawn mowers, sewing machines with televisions, kitchen chairs with bicycles. Baskets and boxes overflowed with bric-abrac — mostly the products of Tod's own fishing expeditions — and over all of it dust lay like a blight.

Beyond the lamp was the door to the corridor which ran between the shop and Mort's living quarters. Both it and the inner door were open so that Tod could see to where the flickering images of the television lit up his father's sitting room. Of Mort himself, however, there was no sign.

Cautiously Tod tried the door of the shop. He was not allowed to come in this way but to reach the back door meant walking right down to the bottom of Old Bridge Street and then round into Rivermarsh Street. Even when he arrived at the rear of the tenement he had three flights of rickety iron stairs to climb on the outside of the building before he again reached shop level. Tonight he felt he simply could not walk any farther.

The door was not locked. Opening it just wide enough to let him in without activating the bell he squeezed his way through and picked his way carefully through the jumble. He was creeping past the counter when he saw, lying beside Mort's old-fashioned till, a neat stack of one pound coins. Immediately his hand shot out to take one. His sudden movement dislodged the carpet on his shoulder and swinging sideways it hit the standard lamp. The lamp tottered, its unfixed shade fell with a crash into a basket full of cups and saucers and at the same time it struck Tod's outstretched arm so that his hand, instead of grasping one, sent all the brassy coins spinning noisily across the counter and over the floor.

"You young devil, you!... Miserable... thieving... no-name runt!"

The words spat from between Mort's teeth in time to the blows he was raining on Tod's shoulders. His handsome face darkened and round the black centres of his eyes the whites were veined with red.

"Devil yourself!", groaned Tod inwardly, "One day I'll kill... I'll kill you..." Chaotic murderous pictures reeled through his head, and he punched the air with his fists. Mort's arms dropped to his sides and he drew back with a laugh. The gold ear-ring he wore flashed with yellow fire.

"Stinking rag-bag!" he said. "Get upstairs... out of my sight!"

Under the eaves of the attic Tod sat on his bed with his arms folded over his head and rocked to and fro. His bruised shoulders throbbed and his head boomed like a cave with echoes of Mort's voice. He drew the back of his hand across his eyes which burned and itched with a dry fire, but there were no tears there. Tod never cried. He never remembered crying... Except once... He stopped rocking and sat very still while the memory came in broken pictures like disconnected bits of a jig-saw puzzle.

Sky so blue it seemed to hurt. The growling murmur of men's voices... Mort in a black suit, his hair swept smoothly back to show the two strange white stripes above his temples ("See that! Twice struck by lightning! Would've killed a lesser man but all it did to me was stroke my hair! You better believe it!") And behind Mort's head a branch of leaves, smudgy green, swaying against the sun... The smell of freshly dug earth... Mort's hand, hard and dry, clutching his... The long pale, satiny box on which lay a ring of red roses... bright as blood...

"Ring-a-ring-a-roses, a pocket full of posies, atishoo, atishoo we all fall down."

The rhyme came lilting into Tod's head and sent the memory pictures scattering. Like someone coming out of a deep, dream-ridden sleep, he stared about him.

The only light in the attic came from the city lights outside, dimmed now by fog as well as by the web of dust on the dormer window. Under the rafters the room was both cold and stuffy and unlike the shop it was almost bare of furniture. Propped against the wall on the far side of Tod's bed was a lop-sided chest of drawers and the bed itself was simply a mattress placed on the floor and heaped with a ragged assortment of coats and blankets. In one corner was the stained enamel pail which served as Tod's lavatory. Up on this floor there was nowhere to wash. Tod rarely washed. Occasionally, Mort, swearing about his stink, would stand him in the downstairs sink and tip a bucket of cold water over him. Tod almost preferred being beaten.

Now, rising stiffly to his feet, swearing and groaning by turns, he shuffled off his coat and crossing to the window he pressed his nose against the blackened glass. Below him the mist washed against the houses like a flood of thin blue-white milk. Tonight the Dream Land was invisible. Turning away he stooped, slid his hand under his mattress and felt for his precious bundle of treasure. Finding it was still safely there he kicked off his shoes and crept beneath the covers of his bed.

"Rock-a-bye-baby in the tree top", sang the long ago, far-away voice in his head, "When the wind blows the cradle will rock. When the bough breaks..."

But before the ribbon of words had fully unwound itself, Tod was asleep.

Chapter 2

Next morning when Tod was on his way back from emptying his slops Mort called him into the shop. Tod set his pail down and slunk into the space behind the counter. The light, filtering through ancient blue paper blinds, was like watered-down ink and it took him a moment before he saw Mort. He was bending over the basket of crockery into which the lampshade had fallen the previous evening. On the counter stood two steaming mugs.

"Get your tea," said Mort, without looking up.

Tod grabbed the battered tin mug which was his, warming his hands before gulping the first mouthful. It was strong and sweet and it made his stomach cramp before sending a trickle of warmth through the rest of him. Mort straightened and Tod saw that he was smartly dressed in a black leather jacket and striped shirt. His sleek black hair was so heavily greased that the livid marks of the lightning were darkened and scarcely noticeable. He took a step towards Tod and Tod shrank back against the wall. Mort grinned.

"I'm off," he said, "on a business trip."

Mort was often away on 'business' trips. He opened the shop only when he felt like it. But whether he was at home or away, Tod was forbidden to go out during daylight hours.

"It's school holidays," said Mort. "Half-term break — or whatever they call it." Choosing a cap from the hat-stand behind the counter he set it on his head at a rakish angle. "Have the day off yourself," he said. "It's Halloween. The day of the dead! Go out and enjoy it." And he grinned again. He was clearly in a good mood. As though the lightning strokes had infected his blood with wayward electrical charges Mort's moods swung wildly. Tod trusted none of them. He took another gulp of tea.

His father raised his foot and shoved the basket of crockery towards him. "But first you can take this lot up to the store and sort out the cracked-and-busteds. Find some new stuff to replace them. And while you're there you can look for a door-knocker. Black iron. Antique. Got a punter wants one."

Tod took the basket handle — it was a large basket of the kind people use to keep firewood in — and dragged it into the corridor. Hastily he swallowed the last of his tea and picked up his pail.

"God you're hideous!" said Mort, following him through the door and locking it behind them. "Look like something the cat brought in. And she must have ate your tongue as usual!"

He loomed over Tod and taking him by the ear he twisted it so that Tod gasped and flinched away — at which he twisted all the harder.

"Keep away from kids," he snarled. "And remember what I told you about the Law! The Law hate mucky little no-name thieves like you. Let them set eyes on you and the next thing you know they'll have you shoved behind bars."

He sniggered, released Tod's burning ear and straightened up. Then eyeing himself in the mirror beside the door he said softly, "They'll take you away and put you in a place that'll make you think this dump was heaven... heaven..." he repeated. "You better believe it!"

The store was in the roof-space on the opposite side of the top-floor corridor from Tod's room. Mort used it for keeping all the goods that had not yet been sorted for the shop as well as for discarded rubbish. Whenever Tod was given the key to do a job like this one, he took the chance of rummaging through the hotch-potch of things and from time to time he risked filching small bits and pieces which he then secreted away with his own treasure.

Today however turned out to be different, a day like no other. For as he was delving to the bottom of the basket for the last fragments of smashed crockery Tod's fingers encountered something small and smooth and round. Withdrawing it he held it to the window where it glinted like gold. He felt it between finger and thumb, spat on it, rubbed it on his jersey, brought it close to his eyes. It did not change or disappear. It really, truly was a one pound coin; one of those he had swept off the counter last night; one that Mort had failed to find.

Tod sat on his bed and nibbled a chocolate biscuit, savouring every bite. When he'd gone out to buy the biscuits the fog had given way to a fine drizzle, but now rain thrummed steadily on the roof and in the corner he could hear a slow thud-thud where water dripped on the floor through a broken tile. He took another biscuit but he knew that if he ate too much too quickly it would make him sick. So he set the rest of the packet, together with the change he'd been given, on the floor between his feet where he gloated over them like a miser with his hoard. He had food — and he had money for more food.

Under his ribs the stone suddenly lightened and the clouds that drifted constantly through his head seemed also to lift and part. Except for Mort's voice and that other one which brought with it words and tunes as if from a great distance, Tod's head was usually blank of everything. Nothing seemed to be there but the basic day-to-day knowledge he needed to keep alive; no thoughts, no ideas, no memories. But when today the clouds parted, something came flittering through like a bird. It was a picture. The picture of a face. A garishly painted face poised above a scarlet bow. A face which seemed to wear a hidden smile just for him.

"Penny for the Guy, Mister?" it seemed to be saying. And then, "Penny for your thoughts?"

Tod was not aware of having any thoughts but, as he leaned over to take a third biscuit, the face did not disappear. It stayed clear and steady in his head and it seemed to him that it was suggesting something to him...

Astonished, he rose to his feet and the face at once vanished. But he remembered it and with an effort he hung on to the idea it had brought with it. Mumbling to himself he walked about the room while the idea grew and grew until it filled his head. He could not say how or why but he knew that the idea was very important. That although it seemed nothing in itself it was like the first unaided step a baby ever takes — everything in what it meant. In a spurt of energy he kicked open his door and going out on to the landing he leaned over the stairwell.

"Yah!" he shouted. "Mort!"

He shook his fist at the empty darkness below and then taking the key from his pocket he unlocked the store-room door again.

Tod made no further use of Mort's permission to go out. He ate his biscuits two at a time rationing them to last while he worked. Even so, with nothing to interrupt him, the task he'd set himself took longer than he expected. The south-west wind which drove the rain against his window also carried the sound of the cathedral clock down to this end of the city and by the time he counted three strokes the light in the attic was already too murky for him to see what he was doing.

He stood up and propped the thing he had been making against the wall. Surrounded by a litter of clippings and offcuts — string, wire, paper, plastic, cotton — it did not yet even begin to match his idea of it. A dingy white ball, made from a pillow case tightly packed with strips of torn sheeting, was wedged into the collar of an all-in-one suit of the kind small children wear in winter. The suit was of fawn waterproof cotton and was patched on one knee with a square of moss green velvet. Tod had plumped out its shape with rags and screwed up newspapers and then to prevent this stuffing escaping he'd oversewn the zipper at the top and stitched the cuffs at wrists and ankles. Finally he'd secured the head to the body by pushing prongs of wire through the fabric of both and fixing them there by twisting the ends together under the collar. Altogether the thing had the look of a rather fat, rather grubby phantom child and dissatisfied, Tod scowled at it.

"Rag-bag!" he muttered.

Then as he blew on his fingers to try and breathe some life back into them there came echoing up through the funnel of the house a great banging, battering sound. For hours he'd been unaware of the outside world. He hadn't even heard the humming of the traffic in the streets. So now the sudden violent noise frightened and confused him and it was some time before he realised what the cause of it must be. Mort was back! He had either forgotten the key to the shop or was too drunk to find it. Whatever the reason he had climbed the iron steps from Rivermarsh Street and was now beating on the back door.

The stone in Tod's chest plunged towards the pit of his stomach as he stumbled down the stairs. But for once he need not have worried. As soon as he drew back the bolt Mort fell through the door and lurching past him as though he was invisible, stood swaying and cursing in the lobby. Dripping water all around him he fumbled with the key to his own inner door and then was gone. Behind him his door swung to but did not close. Tod heard him crash into his bathroom at the far end of the corridor and then there was silence.

The tightness in his chest eased. He knew that Mort would now sleep for hours and by the morning would remember nothing of the night. So this evening he would not have to go fishing and nor did he need to go hunting for food because once Mort was soundly asleep he could sneak into his quarters through the unlatched door and take what he could find from the kitchen. What's more he could carry on with what he was doing because he could borrow the light bulb from the lamp in the shop.

Dazed by the strangeness of the day Tod stood staring at his feet for a moment before he slipped off one shoe, pushed it between Mort's door and its frame, and then went back to his room.

Chapter 3

Comfortably full of bread and milk from Mort's fridge, Tod sat on a broken-backed wooden bench in the car park behind the new shopping precinct. Here, on the west side of the river, he could see the Dream Land again. Yesterday's clouds had vanished and in the clear morning sun the humped green hills looked so close that he had the feeling they'd crept up on the city overnight. Turning reluctantly away from them he looked down at the guy which sat upright beside him. Its head was drooping and he yanked it straight before taking out an old tobacco tin and placing it on the seat between them.

An early shopper coming to the nearby ticket machine, glanced at the guy and with a startled expression glanced again.

"Penny for the Guy," croaked Tod in his husky, unpractised voice, "Penny for the Guy."

The man threw him a coin, hesitated as though he was going to speak but then drifted away. More shoppers came and went. A few dropped pennies into his tin but most ignored him. Then a man in a sheepskin coat approached. As he took his ticket from the machine he was joined by a smartly-dressed woman with a labrador dog. The dog sniffed around the base of the machine while the woman looked keenly at Tod and his guy.

"Hey, David," she said. "Have you noticed this guy? Extraordinary!".

"Hm," said the man. "Not quite the usual sort of thing certainly." And standing close together, they went on staring. Then another person joined them — and another — and soon a small crowd had gathered.

"Did you make the guy?" someone asked Tod.

The people pressed closer, peering at the guy, discussing it, touching it even. Tod was frightened. He wanted to leap up and run away. But he sensed that there might be money in this. He picked up his tin and shook it and at once people began to delve into pockets and purses. Copper and silver coins started to clatter into the tin and then the smart woman dropped a brass coin among the rest.

"If I were you," she said, "I'd make another guy for burning on November 5th. Something rather less... something less..."

Without finishing her sentence she took the man's arm and said into his sleeve, "Odd little bod! I can hardly believe he made that! He's more of a... more of a guy... than it is!"

The words, echoing the words of the boys on the building site, were muffled but Tod heard them. Cheeks burning, he spat like an angry cat and then clamped the lid on his money tin and slid it into his pocket. The woman looked shocked and someone else said, "That's no way to behave, son! You might at least say thank-you!" The mood of the crowd changed. There was a general mutter of disapproval and Tod felt that at any second someone was going to reach out for him... seize him... take him to...

There was a sudden commotion as a lorry loaded with crates of bottles rattled into the car park. Horn honking it drove towards the crowd which was blocking its way and as the people scattered to let it through their ill-temper was re-directed at the driver. Jeering, unconcerned, he pulled up at the loading bay and the crowd, interest in Tod now lost, began to disperse. Only the labrador dog, briefly astray from its owner, came snuffling over to him and prodded his hand with a cold wet nose.

"Get lost!" hissed Tod and lashed out at it with his foot. As it yelped away from him he grabbed his guy and scrambled over a low wall behind him. Finding himself in an alleyway cluttered with dustbins and bursting sacks of rubbish, he crouched out of sight between two bins and slowly recovered his breath.

Squatting against the wall Tod supported the guy on his knees so that its face was level with his own and examined it closely. What was it that had so impressed the woman — and drawn the crowd?

Under a shaggy fringe of thick black hair the guy's face had the chubbiness of a young child's. He'd made the hair from a piece of fur fabric that had once been a lady's evening cloak and the fur was long, silky and so shining black that in the sun it glistened with blue lights. It was stuck down with the strong glue which Mort used for repairing carpets and under the heavy eyebrows Tod had used the same glue to attach two forget-me-not blue flowers. He'd cut the flowers from a scrap of material he kept among his treasures and he noticed now that their purple centres gave the 'eyes' a brooding, thoughtful look. But it wasn't this which troubled him as he gazed at the guy. There was something else... something which teased and eluded him. Growling under his breath he ran his finger over the rosy pink triangles he'd crayoned in beneath the eyes, over the bow of narrow scarlet ribbon he'd stitched on for a mouth, over the white pom-pom of its nose. But still he could not see.

Seizing the blue and white spotted neckerchief knotted over its collar Tod brought the guy's face so close to his own that all its features were swallowed up into the blue of its eyes.

"Blasted, witchy, whey-faced bi..." he began. But his teeth clamped shut and he couldn't continue. For the ugly words had revealed the truth to him.

His guy was not a guy at all... but a girl!

How had it happened? How? When he hadn't intended it and didn't want it? Angry, upset, perplexed, he lowered the guy to his knee again and this time it was the upturned face itself that enlightened him. For whatever he had intended he saw now that in some mysterious way, *the face was right.*

When in the freezing dusk Tod came back to Rivermarsh Street, his pockets were heavy with the money he'd collected. The minute he reached his room he threw the guy into a corner and sat down to count it. Nearly five pounds. A fortune! Grunting with unfamiliar pleasure he wrapped the coins in a piece of rag and stuffed them into a hole in his mattress. All except fifty pence which he slipped back into his pocket.

Where his father discovered it.

Still hungover when he went to get his lunch, Mort had nevertheless noticed that food had been taken from his fridge. He'd gone raging up to the attic only to find that Tod was not there. Out himself all afternoon, as soon as he came in he dragged Tod down to the lobby where he beat, shook, and finally up-ended him. At once the money rolled from Tod's pocket and Mort's rage turned as icy as the air.

"Sneakthieving son-of-a-witch... I don't know why I keep you... you're not worth the stinking air you breathe. Starting to bite the hand that feeds you are you?... Sticky-fingered little swine that you are..."

Abruptly he let Tod go and stooping to retrieve the fifty pence he dropped it into the till from where he swore it had been taken.

"You put another foot wrong," he said, smoothing back his hair with both hands, "and I'll think twice about giving you house room."

His eyes gleamed as though he had lighted upon an idea that excited him.

"Yeah!" he said, lowering his head and speaking very distinctly. "You bring in a good catch tonight, No-name, or the Law can have you tomorrow. I swear it... the Law... I'll hand you over myself!... And you better believe it!"

While Tod cowered against the wall Mort gave him rapid directions and instructions about where he was to go fishing that night. Then reminding him of what he would do if Tod failed, he took him by the seat of the pants and flung him out of the back door.

On the grating at the top of the iron stairs Tod hugged himself and groaned. He did believe what Mort had said. For of all the dreadful things his father had threatened to do to him, that was the worst. What's more, he had never said it before.

Chapter 4

It was still dark when a motorbike, droning like a giant wasp along Rivermarsh Street, jarred Tod awake. He felt sick and dizzy and was swept by a feeling of terror. There was something he'd forgotten. Something he must do. He tried to stand up but his legs kept buckling under him like the legs of a newborn animal. Then his hand, groping for support, swept the guy off his mattress and as it flopped across his feet he remembered...

When he had returned home at midnight he'd been empty handed. Faint with hunger and weariness, his father's threats pounding in his head, he'd lost his way in the labyrinth of streets where Mort had sent him and had found nothing. There'd been no 'good catch'. No catch at all...

With an effort Tod stood upright and began to move about the room. Slowly his head cleared and his strength revived. He had no idea what the time was and the fear that he'd left it too late to do what he had to do drove him to a flurry of activity. From his chest of drawers he took a canvas bag of the kind fishermen use to carry their reels and their bait. He'd often used it for his own very different fishing but now he collected string, scissors, a knife, socks and flung them all into it. Taking his money from its hidey-hole in the mattress he pushed that too into the bag. Then kneeling on the floor beside his bed he humped the mattress on to his shoulders and swept his hand along the boards beneath it until he found the package which contained his treasure. His cold fingers made hard work of opening it but at last it lay spread before him.

Some things he at once discarded. The rest he laid one by one beside his guy. A pocket torch; two new batteries; a box of Swan matches; a mirror, its glass cracked and speckled but its pretty frame of china leaves and flowers intact; an exercise book half-full of carefully printed writing done with a pencil; a lemon yellow jumper, its pattern matted, its size much shrunken and — most precious of all — a small, gold heart-shaped locket. This Tod held tight in his hand while he examined the others.

The first three items had been stolen at different times from the stationer's shop in Old Bridge Street. The mirror had come from Mort's store and never been missed. Only the last three things were truly his. These he had always had. He once had known by heart the faded stories in the book. The yellow jumper had been... had been... he couldn't remember... but he knew he had worn it himself before it became too small. As for the locket... Tod stroked its smooth, warm gold. In the cleft of the heart was a loop where a chain should have been threaded. But the chain was missing. He pressed the little clasp in its side and the heart sprang open to reveal on the inside of each half, lines decoratively engraved in the gold. In the weak light from the street lamps he couldn't see them clearly. But he knew exactly what they were. They were the letters 'L' and 'S'.

Remembering with a start his need for haste, Tod snapped the locket shut and slipped it into his pocket. Then sitting on the floor he picked up the guy and started to tug the yellow jumper over its shaggy head. Stitched inside the neck of the jumper was a label. As he pulled it round to its correct position at the back the word on the label shimmered as if it were printed in luminous ink. Tod spelled it out, M..I..M..O..S..A. He glanced from it to the face of the guy; the pretty face; the girl's face. The brooding flower eyes seemed to meet his own.

"Mimosa," he said. And there it was. It was her name.

"What are little girls made of? What are little girls made of? Sugar and spice. And all things nice. That's what little girls are made of."

The words stole through his head as he added a shabby denim jacket and jeans to the guy's clothing. Scowling he rolled up the hems of the jeans and then letting her fall back on to the bed he picked up the mirror.

Out of its tarnished silver his own face peered back at him, sharp-nosed, ferrety, like the face of a hungry animal. In the cracked surface he could not see himself whole or clearly. But what he noticed was his hair. Scuffed everywhere into knots it straggled over his eyes and hung in ragged elf-locks to his shoulders. With a curse he took the scissors from his bag and began to snip and saw at the sticky tangles. When he was satisfied that there were no long strands left anywhere he threw the scissors back into his bag together with the mirror and the rest of his treasures.

He was ready. And as if on cue he heard the striking of the cathedral clock. One-Two-Three-Four. Good. It was not as late as he'd feared. Pulling a second tatty sweater on top of the one he was already wearing, he slung the canvas bag across it and put on his coat. Then from among the rags of his bedding he took a long black scarf and wrapping it diagonally about the guy and himself, he bound her to his front with her face just beneath his chin. He stood and listened for a second. Except for the creaks and shivers of its old timbers the house was completely silent. Tucking his shoes under his arm, he crept out of his room and down the stairs. Outside Mort's door his breath tightened unbearably around the stone in his chest, but the back door opened noiselessly and, edging round it, he drew it gently to until it locked.

On the bottom step of the iron stairs Tod sat down to put on his shoes. Then hitching up his layers of clothing he slid his hand into his trouser pocket to get his house key. But as well as the key his fingers found the golden locket he'd put there earlier. He brought it out and it lay light and warm on his palm. It wouldn't be safe in his pocket. It could too easily be lost from his bag.

He needed to put it in a place where it would be really secure.

His fingers clumsy from cold and fear Tod loosened the sling which held the guy and pushed her clear of himself. He undid the strong safety pin with which he'd fastened the front of her denim jacket and slipping the point through the loop of the locket, he raised her mimosa jumper and pinned the locket directly to her chest.

As the pin clipped shut a tremor seemed to run through the limp doll body. His cold hands felt it. Warmth flowed up and around his finger tips. At the same time his ears, straining for other sounds, caught the faintest sigh of an indrawn breath and he saw — or thought he saw — Mimosa's blue petal eyes flicker beneath their heavy brows. He wrenched his hands away as if they had been scorched and buried her face against him as he tied her tight again.

Minutes later he stood on the path which ran along the river bank. Raising his arm he threw the key to his father's house far out over the darkly glittering water. It flew in an arc, catching the light from the city's lamps as it dropped. He listened for the splash. But instead, rising up from somewhere just below him, he heard a faint musical droning, a crooning sound. Head bowed he stayed where he was while the sound grew stronger, shaping itself into a tune. And inside his head words began to gather and thread themselves along it.

"And I would love you all the day," went the words, "Every night would kiss and play... If with me you'd fondly stray... Over the hills and far away..."

The song sounded happy, but the feeling it gave to Tod was one of terrible sadness. For he both knew it and did not know it. He felt it had once been part of himself but the self it belonged to was utterly lost to him.

The crooning died away. A chilly breeze breathed up from the water. Tod turned his face away from home and began to trudge along the river path.

PART II

Mim

Chapter 5

Within the first half-hour of setting out Tod discovered that having the guy strapped to his front meant that her feet flapped against his knees and hampered his walking. So he stopped and transferred her to his back. Now her head bounced against his shoulders and her hair tickled his ear but it was much more comfortable. Also the breeze beside the river had become a steady wind blowing upstream and Mimosa sheltered him from the cold of it.

The night was very cold. The moon had set but the sky was like a daisy field, white with stars. To his left the river babbled noisily in its concrete straight-jacket and all around him the lights of the city stared and blinked like thousands of watchful eyes. He had to escape from the city. From the city and Mort and the Law.

He hurried as much as he could but his legs felt weak, his stone burdensome and the riverside path seemed to stretch endlessly ahead. Sometimes it ran along the backs of garden fences, sometimes under the lee of high brick walls guarding factories and warehouses, sometimes through playing fields and stretches of scrubby wilderness.

It was as he was trudging through one such place that he heard a noise — small but persistent — which seemed to be accompanying him. It was a kind of zizzing sound as though someone was blowing softly and tunelessly through their teeth. Tod slowed down, glancing uneasily around him. He could see nothing except the trees, hear nothing except the wind mimicking the sound of water among their branches. He pushed off the hood of his duffle coat so that he could hear better but as it dropped back and fell over the guy's head, another, different sound startled him. Faint as a distant whisper, it nevertheless seemed to come from right beside him.

"Aah!" it seemed to say. And then "Sheesh!".

The cold wind nipped at his shorn head and with a snarl he dragged his hood back.

"Gerroff," he grunted, "whoever you are! Stop bugging me!" There was a short, hoarse, rasping sound as though someone unused to laughing had tried to laugh. Then there was silence.

Tod plodded on. Hunger was beginning to gnaw at him again. Wearily he climbed steps which took the path to the top of the embankment where, looking about him, he could see that the stars had disappeared and the darkness was thinning out. Lights were beginning to come on in house windows. People were getting up. It was morning.

Then from an entry twenty paces away, a man in dungarees appeared and came whistling towards him. Hastily Tod stepped off the path and pretended to be staring into the river.

"Morning!" said the man. "Bit nippy for fishing isn't it!"

He laughed but didn't pause in his jaunty walk and as his whistling ebbed away a tiny echo of it seemed to be left behind. It was the zizzing which had troubled Tod earlier. He shook his head to try to free himself of it but his movement dislodged his hood again and the wind lifting Mimosa's black fringe brushed it against his cheek. At the same time there came once more that sound like a coughing laugh, followed by a voice saying, "Tod... Tod." Or perhaps it was "tired". It was difficult to tell because the voice was husky and rather thick and it spoke the word like a child just learning to talk. "Tod..." it repeated, "... tired... Tod... tired."

"Shut up!" said Tod, "Shut up! Shut up!"

There was a pause but then the voice started to mumble through a sequence of meaningless syllables as if searching for a word it wanted but couldn't pronounce.

"Mim... mim... mim... mim..." it drawled.

Tod covered his ears with his hands but he could still hear the voice going on and on. He wrenched at the scarf which bound the guy to him until it loosened and she lolled sideways.

Seizing her by one padded arm he brought her round to face him. In the dawn twilight, her eyes were without colour, dark and unfathomable. But they seemed to stare pertly back at him.

"Tod," she said. And the red bow of her mouth moved.

He wouldn't believe it. But still it frightened him. The disbelief and the fear together filled him with fury. He swung his arm back so that she dangled in the air and summoning all his strength he prepared to hurl her into the water.

"No!" she said, legs and arms flapping. "No... no... no!... November!"

The last word, coming out clear and true, shocked Tod into a moment's hesitation.

"Mim... Mim... me... member," she gabbled. "Penny... pennyforthe guy... legs in... legsinbumfer... headinsky."

Slowly Tod lowered his arm. He was shaking so violently that in his grip Mimosa appeared to nod and jerk like a dancing puppet. He hated her. But he needed her. That was why he had brought her. She could bring him 'pennies for the guy'; and the pennies would buy him food. For four more days she was necessary.

He did not fling her in the river. Instead he drew back his other fist and slammed it into her face. Then bundling her round and round with the scarf he threw her, head down, over his shoulder and went back to the path.

In the growing light he could see now where the path was going. Fifty paces ahead it skirted a patchwork of allotments enclosed behind a high wire fence. Where there were allotments there might be food and there might also be a shed where he could shelter and sleep. He was so tired that even as he walked his eyelids were beginning to droop.

Behind his back he thought he could hear watery, snuffling sounds as though someone very close to him were crying. He started to hiss through his own teeth, louder and louder until his was the only voice he could hear as he reached the wire fence and began to work his way along it, looking for a place where he could break in.

The clear cold weather held and sunny days were followed by frosty moonlit nights.

In the corner of an unkempt plot on the edge of the allotments Tod had found shelter in an abandoned hut. Surrounded by a thicket of dusty docks, nettles, and trailing brambles, its corrugated iron walls sloped, its door slumped on one hinge and rust had gnawed ragged holes in its roof. Inside it was damp, the earth floor squelchy, and it smelled of mould and rot. Beneath his makeshift bed — a broken table top left by some previous tenant — a colony of woodlice, grey as the earth itself, came and went in perpetual motion.

Like a furtive wild animal Tod slept by day and came out only when the early dusk had driven the last gardener from the allotments. Then he strapped his guy to his back and set off into the streets. Whenever he found a likely place, a street corner, a bus stop, a factory gate, he checked the road for policemen and then swaddling her in the black scarf in case her face should draw attention, he sat her on the pavement and begged pennies for the guy. Haunted all the time by the fear of Mort finding him he didn't stay anywhere long but moved on constantly.

He bought food early, using small shops where he could sometimes pocket a bar of chocolate or a bag of crisps without paying for it. This kind of food he stowed away for his day-time eating but later in the evening he bought chips or a jumbo sausage and once, from a street stall, a baked potato dripping with butter. He never used the same shop twice. He drank water from the tap on the allotments and after having fished an enamel mug out of a workman's hut, he kept it always full in his shelter. By his usual standards he lived well and was rarely hungry.

He slept fitfully, disturbed during the late hours of the night by the cold and during the day by the allotment noises; spades striking stone, water running into cans, voices exchanging greetings. But sometimes as he woke he would think he heard a voice singing softly, fragments of melody which melted away into the silence as soon as he was fully conscious. Or it would seem that someone had spoken to him, the words lingering in his head for a moment or two before the outside sounds dispelled them. When this happened he refused to look at his guy.

To keep Mimosa dry he had placed her on the end of his table-top bed but with her face to the wall so that he could not see it. Once, tossing restlessly because he could not sleep, he kicked against her so that she overbalanced and fell down beside him. Then on the other side of the wall — he was sure it was on the other side — he heard someone say, "Oops! Oops-a-daisy", and sneeze twice. There was a sniffly little laugh and the same voice whispered, "Atishoo, Atishoo, we all fall down."

Tod lay rigid staring at the wall and for one headspinning moment he saw the rusty grey corrugations shimmer like a television screen and as though part of the wall had dissolved away he found himself looking, as if from a great distance, into a square of sunlit grass and shining yellow flowers. The flower heads were shaking, sifting out a fine golden dust which sprinkled over two brown legs... over a white skirt spread on the grass...

Tod shot upright but before his outstretched fingers could touch it the wall had solidified again and his nails scraped painfully against its rough ridges. As his hand dropped down it came to rest on Mimosa's chest. Through the layers of her clothes a tiny throbbing fluttered against his fingers. He drew his hand away, but slowly this time. And instead of sitting her back with her face to the wall he left her lying beside him. For a long time he gazed at the place where the picture had been.

"What are you?" he whispered at last. And then, after a pause, "Who?"

There was no answer. Tod scratched his itching, aching head and lay down again, curling up tight away from her.

Against his back he could feel a shadowy warmth.

"Mim?" he said.

"Mm... hm," someone murmured. "Mim."

Chapter 6

"This is the one o'clock news for today, Thursday, the 5th November."

The radio voice was very close. Loud enough for Tod to hear through the drumming and pinging of the rain on his tin roof. Huddled up in the one corner which was still dry he listened for a moment and then put his eye to a small hole in the back of the shed.

A boy was sheltering under the hedge which bordered Tod's plot. He stood supporting his radio against a tree trunk as he twiddled the knobs and extinguished the news. Music blared out. Satisfied he leaned back, cradling the radio like a baby, and began to whistle. Tod watched him until the beat of the music, merging with the beating of the rain, lulled him into an uneasy doze from which he awoke with a jolt when a whole gaggle of voices, laughing, shouting, broke into his sleep.

His breath tightened around his stone and he put his eye to the hole again. Five or six children were now gathered in the lee of the hedge. They were talking excitedly and as the first boy switched off the music Tod heard one of them say, "'Stoo wet. Let's leave it." The radio boy shook his head and there was more fast talk.

"...Won't take long," said a girl, "and anyway whose afraid of..."

"But wood and everything'll be soggy as my socks in this piddling rain..." said a boy. "Bonfire won't burn the guy — it'll drown him!"

There was laughter, a lull in the argument. The children milled about under the tree and Tod could no longer hear what they were saying. His eye began to ache and he was just about to withdraw when to his horror the first boy gestured towards his shed and like a flock of birds they all swooped from the hedge and disappeared. He could hear them however, trampling alongside the hut wall, drawing their fingers over its ridges, adding yet another beat to the rain. And then he heard them at the door.

There was no escape. The door shuddered as someone pushed at it and it jammed on the threshold. Like a rat cornered Tod drew back, snarling. His movement rammed Mim against the wall behind him and she was squeezed upwards with her head flopping across his. As the door juddered slowly open her black scarf unwound itself and fell down over his face and chest. For a second he was so paralized with fear that he didn't move, even to brush it aside. In that second the children's voices broke into the hut, gonging around the tin walls...

"Pooh!..."

"Cor!..."

"The stench!"

"Smells like a drain..."

"... a stink bomb..."

"... the school bogs!"

... and just as suddenly retreated from it, thinning into coughs and splutters in the open air. There were more shrieks of laughter and cries of disgust and then the thudding of footsteps as the children departed. They hadn't seen him! The darkness of the hut and the blackness of Mim's scarf had hidden him during the brief moments it took his smell to drive them away.

"Sheesh!" murmured Mim.

Tod ignored it. The children had left the door wide open and he could see them now half-way down the allotments, trying the doors of other sheds and when they found them locked, moving still further away. As he watched them Tod knew he could not stay. It was too dangerous and too wet. The water splashing through the holes in the roof and streaming down the walls, was turning the earth of the hut floor to a grey sludge. Soon even his bed would be swamped. But where could he go? And how could he survive when already it was Bonfire Night

and he could no longer collect money with...? The questions —
frightening and unanswerable — swarmed in his head.

"Thursday," he mumbled. "It's already Thursday..."

"Thursday," said Mim, "Thursday's child has far to go."

Tod stared at her. It was the first time she had put words
together like that — in a meaningful way. But still he resisted
knowing that she had spoken. Hunching himself away from her
he sat rocking, trying to think.

"Thursday's child has far to go... Thursday's child has far to
go..." repeated Mim and she began zizzing again, humming "Over
the hills and far away" until he could stand it no longer and went
outside.

The rain had eased to a fine drizzle and the air was warmer
than at any time since he'd left home. It was nearly dark and
there was no sign of the children, no sign of anyone on the
allotments. From a nearby plot he took a cabbage and a swede
and washing the earth off them he put them into a black plastic
bin liner he found among the litter blown against the wire fence.
After that he went back to the hut and emptying his tin of coins
he divided them between his pockets and his fisherman's bag.
Then snatching Mim's warm scarf from under her he folded it
across his chest before putting on his coat.

Mim herself was of no further use to him. She could earn
him nothing now and carrying her would only burden and hinder
him. So he left her sitting on his bed, her face pale in the gloom,
her wide eyes staring after him. As he stepped away from the
door he could feel their gaze still on his back and under his ribs
his stone seemed to twist with a dull protesting pain.

"Why should I care?" he muttered. "All you are is a bundle
of old rags!" And grinding his teeth together he went on.

He went down to the river. Swollen with the recent rain,
the black water churned past him. It came, he knew, from the
hills. From the Dream Land. If he turned left it would lead him
once more into the city, down to Rivermarsh Street, back to Mort.
If he turned right it would take him out... up... over the hills...

Tod turned right.

He had walked about half a mile along the bank when he came to the parapet of a bridge which carried the railway over the river. Beyond the bridge he could see a vast empty darkness with here and there a glimmer as small as a night-light where an isolated house stood among the fields. But there was no way through. The path ended here. A notice on the parapet warned of DANGER and forbade people to cross the railway tracks. And as if to reinforce that warning Tod heard the two-tone blare of a train's siren as it came hurtling out of the darkness towards the city. He kicked against the parapet as the train, braying again, thundered by deafening him. Sinking to the ground he lowered his head until it rested on his knees. Inside it, as if triggered by the movement, Mim's tune started up again.

And it was then that he remembered. He had left his locket — most precious of all his treasures — pinned to her chest.

When at last Tod found his way out of the city it was as though he were a refugee leaving a place under fire. Behind him the night was loud with the bangs and whooshes of fireworks and everywhere the flames of Bonfire Night lit up the sky.

As he entered the dark, unfamiliar world of the countryside he was glad in spite of himself that Mim was there, that in the end he'd had no choice but to take her with him, because he couldn't remove his locket from her chest. The strong safety pin had rusted solid and wouldn't open. When, back in the hut, he'd taken out his scissors and approached her to cut it loose she had screamed on a high, terrified note, almost but not quite out of his hearing, and drops of moisture had oozed from her petal eyes. His hand had trembled so uncontrollably that he could not. He simply could not do it. So he'd pushed her inside the black plastic bag with the cabbage and the swede and slung her once more on his back.

And it was she, not he, who seemed to know where they were going. "Far away," she insisted. And "Over the hills."

In the days that followed however, Tod doubted that he would ever reach the hills. Although sometimes they looked so close that a day's trudge would take him there, at others they seemed so distant that they might have been in another country. Keeping well away from roads he struggled across ploughed fields or squelched along hedge bottoms, so that as the heavy autumn rain persisted he began to take on the colours of the earth itself — brown, rust, black, bronze. His shoes, coat and trousers were caked and splotched with mud. Only Mim inside her black plastic bag stayed largely dry and clean.

The rations he carried were soon gone and once again he was often hungry. He raided gardens for raw vegetables, found shrivelled apples in orchards, hazel nuts and wizened blackberries in the hedges. Occasionally, when desperate, he bundled Mim up in his filthy coat, pushed her into a hiding place beneath a hedge and made for the nearest village where he bought supplies from a shop before returning to collect her.

Then one day as he was walking across lonely, open country the rain and the early dark came down on him before he had found a place to settle for the night. A cold wind drove the rain against his face, making his head ache. His sodden coat clung to his legs and from her plastic bag he could hear Mim's muffled voice complaining up at him.

"Rain... rain... go... away..." she chanted in time with his plodding footsteps. "Come... again... a... nother... day... rain... rain...", keeping on and on until he thumped her and she fell silent.

He began to work his way through a copse which formed a narrow wedge in the angle where two lanes met. The spindly trees were already bare of leaves and there was no shelter there. But as he emerged from it he saw that between the wood and the high hedges of the lanes there was a grassy clearing in which stood a caravan. Warily Tod backed under the trees again but the caravan had no light in its windows, looked decrepit and deserted. He waited and listened but apart from the dripping of the rain and the moaning of the wind in the trees there was no sound. Sure at last that there was no-one there he walked out into the clearing and crossing a rutted track which led into the lane he climbed the caravan steps and tried the door. It was locked.

Retreating, he considered the space under the caravan. The gap was narrow but at least in there the rain would not get at him. Ducking under the steps he crawled into it. Inside the earth was dry and dusty. It smelled of mice and something else, more rank, he didn't recognise. He crawled further in and a drift of dead leaves crackled beneath his knees. In his relief at being out of the rain he whispered to Mim.

"Don't stand up — whatever you do!"

She gave a little choked-off snigger and Tod realised that for the first time he could ever remember, he'd made a kind of joke. Gradually he relaxed. The bed of leaves felt soft and even a little warm. He lowered himself on to it, sank down into it and in no time was asleep.

The grinding of a car's gears woke him. Then two beams of light poked under the caravan, stroking over him where he lay before snapping off as the car's engine died. Tod sat up in alarm and hit his head on the caravan floor.

"Ooh! Ouch!", said Mim whose head had also struck it.

There was a moment's silence before he heard the bang of a car door followed by a woman's squeal of laughter. Tod sat scrunched up in a ball as the beam of a torch swung erratically across the grass and footsteps approached the caravan. High heels tapped up the steps and a key scraped in the lock. Then the door crashed open and someone who sounded as heavy as an elephant pounded over the floor. Tod unclenched his stiff legs. For several minutes everything went quiet and he was just easing himself down into the leaves again when he heard Mort's laugh. Clearly, unmistakeably, unbelievably. And if by any chance there could have been someone else in the world with a laugh like that, it was followed at once by his father's gravelly voice shouting, "Hey Sal! We got him! We got that... rat... caught him right and proper... come here and see... you better believe it!"

Chapter 7

Tod fled. Scrambling out from the far side of the caravan he flung himself through the nearest gap in the hedge and at once began to run. The swishing of the rain, the gasping of his own breath, Mim's groans as she bounced against his back, blotted out any sounds of pursuit but he was convinced that at any moment he would feel the weight of Mort's hands on his shoulders... Head down, stumbling through tussocks of long grass, he charged blindly on until he came to the top of a small rise and crashed into a wooden fence.

The fence was high and slippery with rain, his arms and legs felt as floppy and useless as Mim's, but somehow he climbed over it. Then before he could stand upright the ground disappeared from under him and in a wild roly-poly he was tumbling over and over like a shot rabbit. Arms and legs flailing, Tod tried to get a foot-hold, to grab something solid but every thing he touched tore away and came with him. Leaves and grass, saplings, stones and clods of earth tumbled around him in a gathering avalanche until, winded and barely conscious, he felt he was going to go on falling for ever. Then with a final violent thrust he was pitched headlong into a place of total darkness.

When he came fully to himself Tod found he was lying half buried in a mound of rubble. It was so dark that he might have been enclosed in a black plastic bag like Mim. Even when he brought his hand so close to his face that it touched his nose he could not see it. Groggily he dragged himself clear of the clinging debris of mud and stones and feeling his way on to level ground, he started to manoeuvre to and fro. But he kept blundering into a wall, bruising his outstretched fingers on the rectangles of the bricks, grazing them on the intersecting lines of gritty mortar. In the absolute blackness he felt the wall was all around him, enclosing him, pressing in on him. He began to be afraid.

Then Mim started to talk again.

At first she was mumbling in that way she had, as if she were trying out words that would not come right. The words floated up into the darkness and something in the darkness took them up and mouthed them back.

"Hee-ya-ya-com-sa-sa-can-an-dl-ta-li-ya-ya-ta-beh-yeh-yed." Her voice grew stronger, overriding the echoes until Tod, understanding at last, realised that he had a weapon against the darkness. He remembered his torch.

The thin beam of light wavered over curving, smoke-blackened walls. Swinging the torch upwards he saw cobwebs dangling like dirty handkerchiefs from a high arched roof. When he lowered it he could see broken spars of timber piled against the base of the walls and beneath his feet, yellowish-grey clinker speckled everywhere with black oil. There were no iron rails but Tod knew he must be in a railway tunnel, disused now and abandoned. When he fell he must have come down the embankment bringing with him the landslide which carried him into the entrance. He turned in a circle until the torchlight played over the heap of rubble which, as far as he could see, reached to the roof. Blocked! But if it was blocked for him it was blocked for Mort too!

"Ha!" he shouted. "You can't catch me now Mort!"

"A-a-a-a," boomeranged the echo, "Aa-ee-ow-Mor-or-ort."

As Tod began to walk through the tunnel his relief at escaping Mort soon evaporated. He was too hungry, bruised and tired to walk fast and the tunnel was an eerie, lonely place. He began to worry about how long it was and how deep beneath the earth. How many tons of rock and clay were balanced on the old brick arch above his head? If he died in this tunnel no-one would ever care. No-one would know...

The hollowness in his stomach rose like a wave until it swept dizzily through his head and he could not go on. Sagging against the sooty wall he sank slowly into a sitting position dragging Mim harshly down the bricks as he did so.

"Ouch", she said. "Lemme out!"

Tod undid the sling and dragged her out of her plastic bag. He stuck the torch into the clinker and sat Mim on the far side of it. Lit from beneath her face under its heavy fringe was just a white mask with black holes for eyes.

"Tell..." she said. "Tell me..."

Her voice, caught up by the echo, lisped and whispered all around them and she didn't go on. At the bottom of his fisherman's bag Tod found one bite of a fluff-covered Mars Bar which he nibbled crumb by crumb, making it last. It revived him a little but now the damp from his coat was eating coldly into his flesh. Shuffling it off he picked up Mim's plastic bag and grimaced across the light at her.

"Why should you have it!" he muttered.

Finding his scissors he cut three holes in the plastic, before slipping the bag over his jersey like a tunic. It reached to his knees. Round it he wound Mim's black scarf and then pulled on his coat again. He was still shivering but gradually warmth crept back into him and resting back against the wall he switched off the torch and closed his eyes. That way the fearful darkness of the tunnel disappeared into the ordinary darkness behind his eyelids.

In the silence he heard Mim speak again.

"Tell...," she whispered. "Tell me a story."

"Don't be stupid!" said Tod.

He heard both her sigh and its echo flutter about the walls.

"Once-pon-a-time," she said, "there was a King." She paused. "You listening?" she said.

"No," snapped Tod.

Stories were for babies. Like the stories pencilled in his book which he only kept because it was his.

"Mm-hm," said Mim. "And there was also a Queen... Now this King and Queen wanted a child... but when at last a son was born...," her words were gathering speed, "... everyone fell a-sighing and a-sobbing because he was all wrong..."

"Wrong?" asked Tod in spite of himself.

"Outside he was all right but inside he was all wrong," continued Mim, gabbling so fast now that the echo could only babble meaninglessly. "There was nothing there, he was as empty as a drum, he had no heart and no soul, he was hollow..."

"Oh-oh-oh," mourned the echo, reasserting itself as she stopped.

"Ya!" snarled Tod under his breath.

"The Queen died of grief and nobody knew what to do... except for one wise woman... and she would not say... For the Prince was too young and the way too dangerous."

"What way? Where?" Tod's questions, dropping into sleep, lost themselves among the echoes but Mim seemed to hear them for she said loudly and with precision.

"... The way... to the House with the Green Door."

"... green... green... door," uttered the tunnel. And there, projected against the blackness behind his eyes, Tod saw it.

It was the door he saw clearly.

It was a very ordinary door of the kind that has two frosted glass panels in the top half and two matching wooden panels in the bottom. Its apple-green paint was chipped and flaked in places and there was a small crack in one of the panes of glass. The only remarkable thing about it was the door knocker. Made of brass and shaped like a fish hanging head down, it lay on the upper part of the door — out of his reach. It shone like gold and the fierce light striking off its bulging eye and off the overlapping edges of its scales, made him flinch away. And at once, as if his movement had broken a spell, the picture shattered. Puzzling over it in his mind, recalling it bit by bit, Tod fell asleep.

"There are many roads but only one way," said the Wise Woman to the Prince, "and that you must find for yourself."

"Silly bit!" thought Tod as he woke to the sound of Mim's voice. "Telling the story while I'm asleep."

He was stiff and sore from his fall. He had pins and needles in one leg, his stomach hurt and his mouth and throat were dry.

He found the torch and switched it on.

"That's better," said Mim. "What's the time?"

Tod shook his head. He had lost all sense of the time. All he knew was that he wanted urgently to get out of the tunnel. Picking Mim up he struggled to his feet and gripping her under his arm he set off again as fast as his shaky legs would carry him.

It wasn't long before he saw that ahead of him the blackness was becoming less solid. In the distance a shaft of golden light lay against one wall of the tunnel and soon after that the way straightened and he could see sunlight pouring in through the tunnel mouth. Putting his torch away he hurried towards it.

He was about twenty five paces from it when the brightness blinked as something large moved across the exit. Tod halted. Beyond the tunnel he could now see the railway cutting between its high overgrown embankments. For a moment nothing happened and then the light blinked again and, silhouetted in the archway, he saw the tall figure of a man, black against the sun.

The stone in Tod's chest lurched into his throat. He stepped back to the wall, flattening himself against it, but the clinker beneath his feet rattled sharply and at once the man shouted something. The tunnel wah-wahed the words down to him, distorting the voice but leaving the message clear enough.

"Come-on-on-out-y-young-de-devil-I-I-know-o-y-there-ere-ere..."

Mort! It must be Mort!

Engulfed in misery Tod didn't move except to bury his head in Mim's middle. He could not bear to see his father standing at the tunnel mouth, waiting there like a dog waiting by a rabbit hole. A metal stud on Mim's jacket was pressing painfully into his cheek and he heard her murmuring but could not listen to what she was saying because already footsteps were crunching and crashing towards them over the loose stones. The noise and its echo filled the tunnel...

It wasn't until Mort's hand fell on his neck and gripped the back of his hood that Tod's fear drove him to action. Then he squirmed and struggled, kicked and bit, but all that happened was that the hand tightened its hold and he was half-dragged, half-carried towards the light. And all the time, in his arms he could hear Mim protesting, "No... no... no"

They were hauled out of the tunnel. Cold dry air stung Tod's nostrils and made him gasp. The brilliant light dazzled him.

"For the love of Mike! Stop all that squawking and pecking. You're harder to hang on to than a fistful of hens!"

The voice rumbling up from somewhere deep inside the speaker had more of laughter in it than of anger. Tod's head jerked back and swivelling round he stared into the eyes of his captor. Eyes that were not brown but blue. A bright, piercing blue. Stunned by the surprise, Tod stopped struggling and continued staring with his mouth open.

"You might well gape!" said the man-who-was-not-Mort. "You young villain!"

He gave Tod a little shake and then straightened him up. "What d'you mean by it, eh?" he demanded.

Tod scowled and tried to look away but found his hood was still being firmly held and he could not.

The man was huge. A giant. Taller and broader than Mort by far! He was quite young and his round, reddish face might have been jolly but for its frown. From beneath a checked cap untidy brown ringlets coiled on to the collar of his leather jacket and his baggy trousers were tucked into enormous green wellingtons.

While Tod trembled and remained silent the man studied him for a moment or two. Then reaching out with his free hand he grabbed Mim by one leg and plucked her from Tod's grasp.

"So!" he exclaimed. "You've been nicking other people's too!"

Holding Mim upside down, her face level with Tod's, he swung her like a pendulum. Tod saw her petal eyes widen and her mouth twitch as if she were about to speak. He clapped his hand over her mouth and tried to tug her free.

"Oh, no, you don't!" said the man, clenching his broad fist

tighter round Mim's leg and giving Tod another shake. In his strong grip Tod wriggled helplessly.

"I haven't nicked anything," he said sullenly.

"But I saw you," said the man. "When I was ploughing up yonder... at least I saw your foxy little shadow... just skedaddling down the embankment..."

"Wasn't me," said Tod.

"And I thought," the man continued, "so that's what he's up to! Stashing 'em away in the old tunnel. I'll catch him nicely." He lowered Mim until her spotted neckerchief trailed on the stones before, with a loud sniff, he went on, "Did too, didn't I! Caught you red-handed! But not with one of mine... With some other poor beggar's scarecrow!"

Mim, whose head was now skewed sideways on the ground uttered a little "Oh" and hastily Tod said, "She's not a scarecrow."

"She!" said the man. "You must be joking." He lifted Mim up, turned her the right way up and looked at her closely. "Good Lord!" he said.

He released Tod's hood at last but gave him too another long, hard look.

"If you weren't so young," he said, "I'd think you were some kind of weirdo! As it is, I guess I owe you an apology."

Chapter 8

"The kids pinched the first scarecrow for their Guy Fawkes Bonfire," explained Ged. "Well — I understand that, I suppose. But when the next two disappeared I thought I'd be hanged if I let them have 'em just for larks! I make 'em too lifelike I guess. But if they don't look real enough the birds just sit on 'em and laugh at me!"

Ged was a farmer, he told Tod; just starting up on his own after working for years for his father. He had offered Tod some of his packed lunch as an apology for having wrongly accused him and they were now sitting on a low wall munching cold bacon sandwiches and drinking hot sweet tea out of a thermos.

The wall formed the boundary of the field through which the old railway ran. Above them the sky was pale, distant, wintry. The clouds which had brought the rain had gone, leaving only a gauzy, white veil across its blueness. It was much colder. A pair of crows, like frayed black rags, flapped across the ploughed land and beneath them a flock of smaller birds dipped and soared, skimming the ground as if in search of something.

"Beggars!" said Ged. "They're after my winter wheat."

Tod shuffled along the wall, putting a greater distance between himself and Ged. As far as he knew all men were like Mort and the farmer's irritation might well be taken out on him. Ged looked across at him, his blue eyes hard and sharp.

"So where d'you live then?" he asked.

His thoughts still full of Mort, Tod mumbled something about living in a caravan.

"Near here is it?" said Ged.

Tod said nothing, afraid now of where this conversation might lead, and Ged who had already decided that he was rather dim-witted said, "I daresay you wouldn't let on anyway... you're mitching from school I suppose..." He grinned, remembering his own adventures. "Played hookey myself, " he said, "many a time. But usually with another lad... not with a... with a blessed rag-doll!"

He looked down at Mim who lay sprawled across the wall between them. Tod looked at her too but her face was blank and her blue eyes, bleached by the strong light to the colour of smoke, gave nothing away.

"And I never went near that old tunnel." Ged went on. "What the devil were you doing in there? Bit foolish y'know... foolhardy in fact! It's at least a mile and a half long... black as a pit... spooky... dangerous too I reckon... The brickwork must be as crumbly as a piece of old cheese! Wouldn't go into it myself for the price of a new tractor!"

He leaned over to take Tod's empty cup and was struck, not for the first time, by his smell.

"By!" he exclaimed. "Your ma's going to wonder where you've been today! You smell like something the dog dug out of the midden! She'll never believe you picked up that pong in school!"

Slouched on the wall, picking shreds of bacon out of his teeth and gazing dully at the ground, Tod looked the picture of misery.

"Hey!" said Ged. "Cheer up! Tell you what... come back to the farm and have a bath. That'll shift the worst of it. You can leave your stinky coat on a hedge somewhere — accidently on purpose like — and the weather'll do the rest. That way you might get away with it!"

Horrified, Tod looked up. He wanted to refuse but Ged beamed down at him in such a friendly way he did not know how.

So, loitering unwillingly, trailing Mim by one arm, he allowed Ged to lead him across the lane into his square, stone farmhouse and finally into a room at the back of the ground floor. "Bit of an ice-box in here, I'm afraid," said Ged. "But there's loads of hot water and if you open the airing cupboard it'll warm it up a bit."

He ushered Tod inside and then left him to solve the mysteries of the bathroom for himself.

What Tod had expected was a cold dowsing under a tap in an outhouse. What he found was a cheerful room whose rough-cast walls were painted bright geranium pink and where the bath, hand basin and lavatory were a clashing peacock blue. From a cupboard in the wall he could hear the gurgle of water and when he opened it there was a gush of warm air and a heap of rainbow coloured towels fell about his head. He stuffed them back inside and jammed the door shut to hold them.

The lavatory was wonderful after weeks of squatting under prickly hedges. Tod sat on it so long that Ged thumped on the door and said, "You all right in there? You're very quiet. I can't hear the water running."

So then Tod found the plug and ran the water until the bath brimmed full and the billows of steam almost blotted out Mim where she sat on a low chair beside it. Throwing off his clothes he climbed in. The heat of the water tingled his toes until he grew used to it and then he lay there lapped to his neck in warmth and nearly asleep. As the bath cooled he made a half-hearted attempt to wash but the soap slithered from his fingers and lost itself somewhere in the murky grey soup the water had become.

"Go on!" said Mim. "Rub-a-dub-dub, three men in a tub!"

Drowsily Tod glanced at her. Through the clouds of steam it seemed to him that she'd grown bigger and that she was leaning forward and smiling. He rubbed his eyes and saw the outline of her face waver uncertainly, its features shift. It was as if she had two faces that were melting into each other. Or as if someone were trying to place a tracing of one face on the picture of another and couldn't quite get them to match. He heard her chuckle but just as she started to say something, Ged banged on the door again.

"Come on lad," he bawled. "You've had time enough to bath a whale!"

Startled, Tod shot up out of the bath spilling water everywhere and splashing it over Mim who at once seemed to shrink back to normal. Then, for minutes, he hopped about the cold floor until he remembered how he should get dry.

He left muddy marks on the tiles and yet more of his dirt came off on the towels. Hastily he pulled on his clothes, the black plastic bag, his coat. On the window ledge was a shaving mirror fuzzed with vapour. He rubbed it clear and stared at his own face. His hair had grown. Darkened with the wet it clung to his forehead and beneath it his skin looked white as paper. But for the first time ever he noticed he had a peppering of brown freckles over his nose and cheekbones and that his rain-coloured eyes had flecks of green in them.

He turned back to Mim and seeing that her nose was smudged with soot he scrubbed it hard with a towel before slinging her across his back and fixing her there with his scarf. As he found the outside door, Ged came along the hall and pushed a banana and a hunk of cake into his hand.

"Keep you going," he said, "till you get home. But don't play truant again. Next time it mightn't be someone as nice as me that catches you!" And with a laugh he pushed Tod out.

Fortunately for Tod he did not go immediately into his bathroom where the bath was still full of scummy water, the soap half dissolved, three blackened towels trampled into the puddles on the floor and half a roll of toilet paper unwound and coming apart in the wet.

Cleaner and warmer than he had been since he could remember, Tod went out into the fields in the keen late-afternoon light, with Mim zizzing 'over the hills and far away' in the teeth of the rising wind.

Chapter 9

The wind persisted. Strong and cold it blew for days on end. It spun the last papery leaves from the trees and swept them into drifts of russet and gold. It dried Tod's coat, turning the splodges of mud on it to scabby crusts which it then blew away as dust.

"Over the hills and a great way off," trilled Mim, "the wind will blow my top-knot off!"

The Dream Land, however, had disappeared again and Tod allowed himself to be thrust along in the direction the wind was taking. Although there were no visible hills he was climbing steadily. The fields grew larger and more open and in the scrubby hedgerows the few sparse trees were bent and crippled by the weight of the air on their backs. In this exposed landscape Tod was constantly troubled by the fear of Mort finding him. Among all his other fears this was the worst. He didn't know who he was. He had no idea where he was going. But he now knew one thing for certain — he did not want to go back to his father. Not ever.

"Listen," said Mim suddenly. "In his travels the Prince came to a land which was ruled over by an Evil Sorcerer."

"Oh no!" groaned Tod. "Not now!"

He was skirting the ruins of an old barn where the wind mourned over the tumbled stones and whistled through the gaps in the walls. He was tired of its everlasting blather but together with the clouds in the sky it seemed to have blown away the clouds inside his head and pictures of the events of the past few weeks kept crowding through it. They'd not been blotted out like everything in the Time Before and he could summon them up whenever he wanted...

"Sheesh!" said Mim, "What's the use of me telling you a story when you don't pay attention?"

Tod scowled at her over his shoulder. But perhaps after all he should listen to her. There were things she seemed to know... things to do with him. And in any case she was all he had...

"Go on then," he said.

"When the Sorcerer's spies brought him news that the Prince was crossing his country he set about making a spell that would bring him to his Dark Tower... And because the Prince was hollow he had no defence against the Sorcerer's enchantment. Like a fish caught in a net he was dragged from his right way and hauled to the Tower — and there he was at once imprisoned in the dungeons."

"I don't think I like this story much," said Tod. He sat down on one of the broken corner-stones of the barn and took half a stale pork pie out of his bag. It was the last of his food, bought with the last of his money. "Why did the Sorcerer want the Prince anyway?" he asked.

"He wanted to fill his emptiness," said Mim.

"Wasn't that a good thing? Isn't that what the Prince needed?"

"Stupid!" exclaimed Mim. "He was an evil Sorcerer. He wanted to fill him full of wickedness."

She paused for a long time as if to let this sink in and through a mouthful of pie Tod said crossly, "Get on with it!"

"Weeks and months and years went by in which the Sorcerer worked on his spells and the Prince in his dungeon never saw the light of day. He grew thin and pale and sadder than sorrow itself."

"Why did it take so long?" asked Tod.

"Mm... Hm," said Mim.

She didn't continue until Tod stood up and brushed the pastry crumbs off his coat. Then she said slowly, "It might have been... because the hollow place inside the Prince was not made for wickedness... And so the Wizard could not find a spell that would really work."

"Didn't he... did he ever try to get away?" he asked.

"He didn't know how," said Mim. "There was no door and

no window in his dungeon. Only a small grille in the wall where his food was put through and where the Sorcerer slid in and out like a shadow."

"So," thought Tod. "That's the end of the story. If he never escaped..."

"I didn't say," said Mim, "that he never escaped."

Many nights later, after trudging for hours under the waning moon, Tod found himself on the edge of a smooth grassy plateau. The grass was raked flat by the wind and there was not a tree nor a bush in sight, only here and there a leafless clump of bramble or briar, thorny and inhospitable. Half a mile off he could see two long, low buildings, grey and featureless in the dawn light. In the whole landscape they offered the only hope of shelter. Wearily hitching Mim higher on his back he headed across the plain towards them.

When at last he reached the first building he stood in the lee of its wall and beat his fists against its cold grey corrugations. For there was no shelter here. Not a nook nor a cranny into which he could creep and rest out of the wind. The buildings were entirely windowless and on the far side where they faced across a wide tarmac strip, their massive doors were drawn across their fronts and securely locked.

Shivering with cold and fatigue, Tod moved out on to the tarmac and stared across it, not sure that what he was seeing could be real. Directly ahead of him, distinct and solid against the flat grey light, the flat grey landscape, stood a diminutive aeroplane. It was so small, so fragile looking — yet so brightly coloured — that it bore no resemblance to the huge metallic machines which Tod often saw plying to and fro across the sky. It looked like an exotic bird that had strayed from another planet. The whole of its cockpit and the foreparts of its wings were painted in swathes of blue, pink, yellow, green, mauve — the bands of colour merging and coiling into scrolls and spirals and circles. From the tarmac a silver ladder led to a black gash in its side, a break in the pattern, where the door had been opened and fastened back against the fuselage.

Tod lapsed back against the wall and closed his eyes. He knew he could not walk any further. In the last twelve hours all he had eaten was a small maggotty turnip and a crust of bread dropped by a bird. But beyond this abandoned, desolate place lay only more barren moorland, scoured dry by the wind.

For how long he stood there unseeing while the wind shook him like a dry stalk he had no idea but when he looked again he saw that the sun was rising. Wisps of ragged cloud smoking up from the horizon were lit with a fiery glow and all around him the light was softening, turning rosy. Across the tarmac the 'plane's winged shadow reached towards him.

"Go on," said Mim.

It was the first time she had spoken for ages and her voice was faint and scratchy.

"Go on where?" asked Tod. "There isn't anywhere..."

"Not here," said Mim. "Over the hills. And far away."

"Stupid!" groaned Tod. "I can't... I can't!"

"Can," said Mim, her voice much stronger. "Must. Thursday's child has far to go..."

Tod reached over his shoulder and yanked her towards him by the hair.

"If you say that once more," he said "I'll... I'll dump you here and leave you!"

Mim made a strange high honking sound and he released her. Her head flopped against his and he pushed it surlily away.

"Don't honk at me," he muttered, "Honking silly old goose!"

There was a short silence. Then Mim said, "Old Mother Goose when she wanted to wander — would ride through the air on a very fine gander."

Tod turned to look at her. Her head lay on his shoulder, her face towards him. The rosy light had warmed its pallor to a healthy pink and her eyes were very blue. As he watched her he was sure that one of them flickered shut in a rapid wink.

"Go on," she said. "Go on."

Chapter 10

Inside the aeroplane was not much bigger than the interior of a car. There were two squat, green leather seats in the cockpit and behind them, on either side of a short gangway, two more. Filling the gangway was a shabby suitcase and on one of the rear seats there was a bulging hold-all with a white anorak thrown over it. As soon as Tod saw the luggage he knew he was in trouble.

"Why did you get me into this?" he hissed at Mim.

"You know," mumbled Mim. "Thursday's child... oops!... and all that..."

"Sheesh!" said Tod.

Mim snuffled with laughter.

Glancing out of the cockpit window, Tod could see that a short distance away a jeep was parked. From where he had stood by the hangars the aircraft itself had hidden it from his view. But now he could also see that there were two people there. Someone was sitting behind the wheel of the jeep and standing beside the window, talking to him, was a young woman. As he stared out at them, fuzzy headed with hunger and weariness, unable to think what to do, the woman turned to face the 'plane.

"Tod be nimble, Tod be quick," croaked Mim. "Tod jump over the candlestick!"

Tod dropped to his knees. Outside he heard footsteps on the tarmac and in panic he scrambled over the suitcase and crawled towards the space between the passenger seats and the back of the cabin. There wasn't much room and he'd hardly had time to shuffle himself into it when the metal steps rattled and from somewhere further off a man called out a single word which sounded improbably like 'legs'. The steps rattled again and then Tod heard the feet going away.

In a strangled voice Mim said, "Let me out of here. I'm as

squished as an old tube of glue."

"Serve you right," snarled Tod. "You silly bit!"

Nevertheless he twisted around in the cramped space until he managed to loosen her sling and drag her forward so that she lay face to face with him. At such close quarters he could see that she was looking the worse for their travels. Her hair was spiked with bits of twig and straw like a badly-made bird's nest. Her nose was grubby where he'd scrubbed at it with Ged's towel and most of the colour he'd crayoned on her cheeks had rubbed off. She looked as pale and scared as he felt.

"What are we going to do!" he said. "I don't know what to do."

"Cock-a-doodle-doo! Cock-a-doodle-doo!" chanted Mim. "My master's lost his fiddling stick and doesn't know what to do!"

She started to giggle and Tod slapped her. Then he pulled the black scarf up and over them both, hiding them as best he could.

"Unless those people go away," he said, "we're trapped."

"Like the Prince," said Mim. "In the Sorcerer's dungeon."

In the stifling blackness under the scarf they might themselves have been in a dungeon. Tod could no longer see Mim but she was rammed so tightly against him that even through their clothes he could feel the pressure of the heart-shaped locket pinned to her chest. It reminded him of the stone in his own chest and he realised with surprise that there were times nowadays when he could not feel it, when he forgot it altogether. Fidgeting himself into a more comfortable position he said,

"Go on then..."

"One day," Mim said, " a mouse appeared in the Prince's cell. A shy grey mouse which scuttled about the floor looking for crumbs. At first the Prince was so sunk in misery that he didn't notice it even though it squeaked and rustled and tickled his feet as it ran over them... Gradually however it dawned on him that something beside himself was there in his prison and though he could barely see the mouse in the gloom, he began to talk to it... even to share his food with it so that it wouldn't go away and leave him."

"Did he like the mouse?" asked Tod.

"Because of his hollowness the Prince didn't understand 'liking'. But any company seemed better than none."

On the other side of the thin cabin wall Tod heard more sounds of activity. He put his finger to Mim's lips and held his breath but the sounds receded and he let her go on.

"Of course," said Mim, "the mouse couldn't talk. But the Prince began to feel that it was trying to tell him something all the same. It ran back and forth between him and the darkest corner of his cell, the corner into which it always disappeared when the Sorcerer arrived. When he didn't respond to that it crouched there squeaking like a rusty hinge until he threw his shoe at it for disturbing his sleep. Finally it laid a trail of crumbs between the Prince's corner and its own and even in the lightless dungeon the crumbs showed up like tiny white pebbles in the dark. At last the Prince paid attention..."

For a few minutes Tod ceased to listen to Mim's husky whisper. In the darkness he was again seeing a picture. But this time he knew it was a picture from a book, a proper printed book he'd seen, long ago, in the Time Before. The picture was of a dark wood where the trees had frightening faces and gnarled arms instead of branches. Very small among the tall trees of the wood were two children, boy and girl, walking hand in hand. And the path they walked along was a line of white stones glimmering in the blackness...

"The mouse made a path," he said. "Like Hansel... and Gretel..."

"Mm. Hm." agreed Mim.

"Then what happened?" asked Tod.

He was so engrossed in Mim's story that he'd forgotten to listen to the sounds outside and it was only when a man's laughter suddenly filled the cabin that he realised the two people had returned and were actually climbing into the 'plane. Mim didn't answer him but went quiet as though she too were listening. He heard the clang of the metal steps, a girl's light voice, the creak the leather seats in the cockpit, the thud of the door being closed.

He began to shake. His whole body trembled, rustling the plastic bag, making his heels knock against the floor. But whatever noise he made was lost as the aeroplane's engine spluttered and stuttered and then grumbled into life.

In terror, half wanting to be discovered and let out, Tod sat up. Between the seats he could see the back of the man's head... headphones resting on a brown neck... hair greased back... a gold ear-ring...

Frozen with shock Tod sat there while the throttle opened up to a deafening roar and the whole fabric of the little aircraft shook and chirrupped. Then faster and faster the aeroplane rolled forward until he felt the wheels lift, the cabin sway and rock... and like a clumsy, unwieldy bird it lurched into the air. For a second he felt sick and dizzy. Then a dreadful pain shot through his head and he knew nothing more.

Tod, who never dreamed, had a dream. He dreamed he was riding on a roundabout, sitting astride a gawky bird, with red-rimmed eyes and a hooked beak. The roundabout was spinning giddily and the bird kept shooting upwards with alarming speed before plunging down with a force that almost unseated him. Around him coloured lights were flashing and popping as though he were whirling in the middle of a firework display and from somewhere nearby loud tuneless music hurdy-gurdied over the fairground.

Then he was wandering among a maze of stalls and fairground rides and in front of him he could see Mim. She was tripping along like an excited child, teasing him by keeping just out of reach.

"One, two, three," she called over her shoulder, "you can't catch me." And whenever he drew close enough to see the gleam of laughter in her blue eyes, she was off again, nipping down a passageway between booths, skipping in and out of the shadows. He could hear himself calling her, "Mim! Mim! Mim!", but each time he spoke her name another voice threw it mockingly back at him. A shiver crawled up his spine and his own cries dwindled away.

Then, strutting out of the darkness into which Mim had just disappeared, came the gaudily painted roundabout bird. It stooped towards him and flashes of white light played over the hooked beak, the reddened eyes, the sleeked back feathers of its head...

Tod felt his voice squeezed from him in a thin high scream and he struggled to wake, to escape. But as the bird lifted one foot there, clutched in its talons, was Mim. Drooping. Silent. Still. From somewhere faraway Tod heard a sigh which swelled like the surging of wind in the trees. He stopped struggling and instead, raising his arm, he aimed a mighty blow at the bird.

"Mort," he cried. "I'll kill you Mort!"

But his hand met only empty air as the bird disintegrated in a blizzard of feathers. The feathers floated gently down, smothering him in a soft, black drift. Half squealing, half choking he thrust them away and found himself, as he came round, wrestling to free his face of Mim's black scarf.

"All the King's horses and all the King's men," whispered Mim sleepily, "couldn't put Humpty together again!"

Slowly Tod remembered where he was. The movement of the aeroplane was smoother and the engine's noise had quietened to a steady thrum. Through it he could hear the murmur of voices like voices on a distant radio. Very carefully he raised his head until he could once more see the people in the cockpit. The woman was invisible behind the back of the seat but the man had turned towards her and without surprise Tod saw that he had a high freckled forehead, a bristling ginger moustache and was not in the least like Mort. Adjusting his headphones the pilot faced forwards again and Tod inched himself up to try to see out of the window.

When he glimpsed the land below he felt his lips stretch and twitch upwards of their own accord and for the first time he could ever remember he smiled. Reaching for Mim he brought her head level with his own.

"Look," he whispered. "The Dream Land!"

"Over the hills," agreed Mim, "and far away!"

And indeed, beneath them were the grey, green and tawny flanks of a range of hills, hump after hump highlighted by the sun, with the long clefts running between them drowned in blue shadow. The plane veered slightly, swinging away from the sun and Tod saw its own faraway shadow skim the last crest like bird.

"Goosey, goosey gander!" remarked Mim jauntily.

Abruptly he let her fall across his knees where she lay face down as the 'plane dropped lower over a patchwork of small fields, a silver thread of river, toy-sized villages. Out of the corner of his eye he saw the pilot turn his head and in alarm he ducked and squeezed himself back into his airless hiding place. His shoulder hurt where it was jammed against something hard and one leg had gone to sleep. He felt the aeroplane wobble as if the wind had given it a friendly shove and then it swooped downwards and he was rammed harder than ever against the back of the cabin, pinned there by the speed of the drop. His ears blocked painfully, his empty stomach churned and he thought he was going to be sick.

"Don't... don't... don't..." begged Mim.

He swallowed again and again and just as he felt he could stand it no longer, the wheels touched down. Once, twice, three times the aeroplane bounced, jolting him until his body felt bruised all over, before it taxied smoothly, at last, to a halt.

Chapter 11

When the noise of the engine cut off, the pilot's voice broke into the silence loud and clear.

"Well, Legs, my love," he said "This is it. You can't see the house from here. It's about a mile away across the park. But there'll be a car coming to pick you up."

"Thanks very much," said the lighter voice of the girl, "That was great — you know I've never flown before so it was a really exciting new experience."

"Glad to oblige," said the pilot. "But what about the new experience ahead of you? You excited about that? Or petrified? Can't imagine why you volunteered for such a thing! Pity your friend couldn't come — she'd have been some support... A friend among the fiends!" He guffawed with laughter and the girl joined in.

"Well, I think it'll be fun," she said, "I'm really looking forward to it.'

"But so many!" he said. "And for two whole weeks! It'd be my idea of..."

He was fumbling with something at the front of the 'plane so that Tod could not hear the rest of the sentence but the girl said, "I think it's a marvellous thing for them to do though — don't you — marvellous, I mean, as a... as a thanksgiving?"

Again Tod could not hear the man's response. There was a lot of movement in the cockpit and the 'plane rocked slightly. Then he heard the metal steps being lowered and clearly again, the pilot's voice saying, "Leave your things... we're a bit early... we'll have a look around the park and I'll fetch them when the car's due."

There were more sounds of movement and scrambled voices and then quietness fell upon the aeroplane.

"Now what?" said Mim.

Tod wasn't sure. He had to escape before the pilot returned for the luggage. Anyone removing the case from the gangway would be certain to see him. He listened hard, trying to decide whether the people had really gone away but all he could hear were the creakings and squeakings of the aeroplane's fuselage as it settled down after its flight. Even the wind seemed to have dropped.

"Go on," urged Mim. "Last one out of here's a purple pig..."

Tod sat up and looked out of the window beside him. Then he crawled across the cabin and looked out of the other side. As far as he could see a smooth carpet of grass surrounded the 'plane in all directions. The grass was enclosed by a white wooden fence and beyond the fence, close up against it, was a high hedge of evergreen bushes. Through a gate in the fence he could see more grass, trees... and strolling towards the gate, in full view of the 'plane, were the pilot and the girl.

"Can't go yet," he said and gathering Mim up he sat on the case in the gangway where, without being seen himself, he could watch the movements of the two people.

"Listen," said Mim. "Listen. In the corner of the Prince's cell the crumbs the mouse had laid down led to nothing more nor less than a mousehole."

"Stupid rag-bag!" he said. "Fancy trying to tell me that now!"

Hoisting her over his shoulder he pushed her into her sling again and tightened the knot on his chest. Her hair tickled his neck and he brushed it away, swearing, but undeterred she went on.

"The mousehole was much too small for the prince — or the Prince was much too big for the mousehole — but the mouse, by constantly running in and out of it, by tugging on his shoe laces, by beckoning with its long, grey tail, seemed to be saying 'This way. This way.' And the extraordinary thing was..." said Mim, nodding against Tod's ear as he saw the pilot reach the gate in the fence, "the extraordinary thing was, that when the Prince gave in and put his nose to the hole, he found he could actually get his head inside, and then his shoulders and then of course the whole of him. Mm-hm! Either the mousehole grew big enough or he shrank small enough but in no time at all he had wriggled and jiggled himself all the way down it."

The pilot and the girl were standing with their elbows propped on the top bar of the gate. They looked settled there. As fixed and motionless as people in a photograph.

"Move," pleaded Tod. "Please, please move!"

"That was what I was just telling you," said Mim. "He did move. He followed..."

"But where?" asked Tod. He was gripping the ends of his scarf with both hands, crushing and crumpling them, willing the man and the girl to move. "Where did the mouse-hole go?"

"It went about and about the Sorcerer's Dark Tower, out under the black moat, out through the woods where the sun never shines..."

Tod saw the man straighten, stretch, walk past the woman and unlatch the gate. "And did he escape?" he asked. "Was he safe then?"

"Almost," murmured Mim, "Al... most."

Both people now had their backs to the 'plane, were turning through the gate, walking away from it. Tod stood up. This might be his only chance. Watching them all the time, he made his way to the door. They were still going away. Stiffly, slowly he lowered himself down the steps on to the cropped turf. He'd spent so long cramped up, gone so long without food, that his legs felt heavy and his head felt light. He knew only that he must find some cover where he could lie low until the people and the aeroplane had gone away altogether.

Bending double Tod started to cross the field. He wanted to run but his feet seemed to creep over the ground. He was about half way between the 'plane and the fence, heading for a place where the hedge seemed thickest, when he heard a shout and glancing to the gateway, saw the pilot standing there waving his arms. His stone banged in his chest but he stumbled on. He sensed rather than saw that the girl had joined the man and making one last effort as he heard their footsteps thudding towards him, he threw himself at the fence and tumbled between the railings. Then groaning with pain he curled into a ball and rolled under the low hanging branches of the nearest bush.

PART III

Legs

Chapter 12

Through the criss-cross of grey branches behind which he crouched, two golden-brown eyes stared at Tod. The girl's face registered first alarm, then amazement and finally amusement. From a short distance away Tod heard the pilot say, "Is he there? Have you found the little beggar?" The girl straightened up and turned round.

"Yes," she said.

While she was facing away from him Tod tried to wriggle out backwards through the bushes but twigs were hooked into his clothes, ropes of ivy twined about his legs and he was trapped.

"I doubt he got near the 'plane," the girl was saying. "He probably spotted us at the gate and ran for cover! Anyway — I'll deal with him."

The pilot said something about it being 'good practice' and then told her he was taking the luggage to the car and she shouldn't be too long. She made a thumbs up sign and leaned over the fence again.

"Hey-up," she said, "there's no need to be so scared!"

She was very tall. Long legs in black tights gangled from beneath a skirt so short it hardly covered her bottom. Tucking them under her she knelt down so that she was on a level with Tod and to his surprise her full lips spread in a smile that seemed to fill her whole face.

"Well, hello Dolly!" she said and reaching through the bars she tweaked Mim's hair.

Tod shuffled back, snarling, and quickly she withdrew her hand.

"I should keep still," she said, "or you'll ravel yourself right into those bushes and be stuck for ever. Hang on a jiff..."

She placed her bulky shoulder-bag on the ground in front

of her and began to rummage inside it.

"You quite scared me at first," she said. "I thought I was looking for one person and there were two faces peering up at me out of this rhody-whatsit... You looked so strange... unreal... it was like finding a couple of... of... goblins... or something..."

All the time she was talking she was rooting about in her bag, shifting a hotch-potch of things this way and that, spilling out bits of its contents and snatching them up again.

"Ha!" she said at last. "Got it!" She held up a pair of scissors.

Tod was still wary but there was something about the girl which made him feel lighter... easier... So although he didn't respond, he didn't try to move away when she half stood and then slid her long legs between the railings and squeezed herself through on to his side of the fence.

"You didn't really have to fling yourself so enthusiastically into this lot," she laughed as she snipped at the ivy and tugged at the branches which ensnared him. "Even if he'd caught you, Nick wouldn't have eaten you... What's your name by the way?"

"Tod," he mumbled.

"Did you say Ted... or Tom?" she asked.

He didn't answer but she didn't seem to notice. She went on talking to him as if he were someone she had known all her life and while she talked the expressions on her face changed constantly as though it were lit from within by a bright but flickering flame. With her head so close to his Tod could see that her short brown hair was coloured with green and silver streaks and whenever she looked up her tawny eyes seemed to catch and hold all the light of the sky. When she dragged away the last branch which held him she waited while he crawled clear and pulled himself upright against the fence.

"There you are," she said. "Unbound!" She stood up and then stooped to pluck dead leaves from her tights. "I'm not certain of the rules yet," she said. "But I'm fairly sure you're out of bounds! You'd better go back. You don't want to be in trouble on the first day, do you?"

Tod drooped against the fence. All strength had gone from

him and he could think of no answers to give to questions he
didn't understand. The girl leaned across him to have a closer
look at Mim.

"Dolly's very unusual," she said. "Though a bit... well...
jaded. Did you make her?" Noting Tod's curt nod she went on
in a rush, "I'm sorry. I suppose you don't like me calling her
'dolly'. Trouble with me is — I speak before I think. But what
exactly is she? I mean it seems rather odd for a boy to have... I
mean..."

She bumbled to a stop as if she was afraid she was going
to say the wrong thing again and from somewhere beyond the
aeroplane came the blare of a car's horn. With a quick, "That's
for me!" she vaulted over the fence. "You look all in," she said
to Tod. "I should go straight back to the house..."

"Legs!" bawled the pilot's voice.

"Wish he wouldn't call me that!" she exclaimed. Then turning
back to Tod, who had not stirred, her face clouded and she said,
"Come on. Climb over the fence and go through the gate into
the park. I don't think it's too far that way..." The pilot shouted
again. "Oh, lord!" she said, "Must go. See you, Ted!" And raising
one hand in farewell she strode away across the grass.

The wind had departed leaving everywhere very still. Over the
trees of the park Tod could see the mountains. Hunched against
the horizon they looked like sleeping dragons, their huge grey-
green flanks softened by a slight haze as though the dragons
breathed out a gentle smoke as they slept.

"Well," he said to Mim. "There are the hills and we've come
over them — so where are we now?"

Mim didn't answer and the silence gathered round them
again.

The park was like no other park Tod had ever seen. There
were no flowerbeds, no ponds, no swings or roundabouts, no
bandstands and no paths. Just grass and trees that seemed to go
on for ever. Wearily he plodded on while unanswerable questions
ached in his head.

Why had the girl — Legs — sent him into this park?... And talked as though that was where he was meant to be?... Where was the house she'd spoken about?... And where — oh where — was he to find food?

He stumbled over a tree root, lost his balance and sank down against the trunk. The bark was smooth and silvery, the wood felt warm, sturdy, comforting. He didn't think he could walk another step and leaning back against it he closed his eyes.

"No," said Mim. "Come on."

Her words were slurred and slow like his own thoughts. Above his head a bird uttered a series of sad, sweet notes and in the following silence Tod thought he could hear, faintly and far away, the sound of voices raised in shouts and laughter.

"Boys and girls," said Mim more firmly, "come out to play."

He opened his eyes and sat up.

"Come on," she repeated. "You find milk and I'll find flour and we'll have a pudding in half an hour!"

"Get lost!" said Tod. But he stood up and staggered on.

The voices drew nearer, grew louder but still he saw no-one. The trees of the park crowded more closely together, became a strip of woodland which in turn gave way to a shrubbery, spiky with thorns, fiery with winter berries. Tod battled his way through and found himself on a broad gravel path which curved away from him in both directions. He couldn't see where it led but turning left and keeping close to the high evergreen hedge on the far side he began to walk along it. He'd only gone a few paces when coming round the corner towards him he saw a small child.

Nervously Tod backed into the hedge. But the child was very young. Warmly dressed in red anorak and trousers he wobbled along on wide-apart legs. As he came closer Tod saw that grasped in both plump fists he held a big crusty roll of bread. The roll bulged with sausage which steamed in the cold air wafting towards Tod the savoury-sweet smell of cooked onion...

The child lowered his head and bit into the hot dog, tearing the bread. Bits of sausage and onion dangled from his mouth as he chewed. Tod stepped out on to the driveway. Looking up, the boy smiled at him out of moist blue eyes. His lips, shiny with fat, curled up and made two deep dimples in his flushed cheeks. He waved the hot dog at Tod in a friendly greeting. With a furtive glance behind him Tod checked that they were alone and then snatched it out of the child's hand. The little boy's eyes grew round as full moons and filled with tears. Opening his mouth he wailed with grief and fury.

"Shut up," said Tod and gave him a push.

The child tottered and keeled over, his legs threshing the gravel as he lay there and bawled. From round the corner someone cried, "What's up, Toby? Have you hurt yourself?" Then two girls, one large, one small, came skidding into sight and Tod fled into the hedge.

Taking the path he found on the far side he crammed the bread and sausage into his mouth. It made his stomach gripe painfully but he hurried on, putting as much distance as he could between himself and the children. Some time later, as he slowed down, he became aware that Mim was zizzing again. When she began to put words to the tune he knew they were words he'd heard sung before, words out of the forgotten past.

"What are little boys made of?" she chanted. "Slugs and snails and puppy dogs' tails... that's what little boys are made of."

Thinking she was referring to the little boy who'd kicked up such an unnecessary fuss he turned his head to grin at her. But with a surprised and sinking feeling he saw that the blue of her eyes was very like the blue of the child Toby's. And that like his too, their brightness was blurred by tears.

Chapter 13

There seemed to be children everywhere. To avoid them Tod had to keep changing direction, turning first one way and then another, following an intricate maze of footpaths. Occasionally in spite of his caution he did come face to face with one or more of them and strangely, although they sometimes glanced at him curiously, none of them showed any surprise at seeing him. They simply carried on playing, chattering, squabbling as if he wasn't there. Once or twice he came across adults too, men and women in green overalls who were trimming the hedges or clearing dead wood from among the trees and shrubs. They also took no notice of him.

"Why?" he said to Mim. "What is this place?... What's going on...?"

But Mim gave him no answers.

For some time he had been walking in the shadow of a high stone wall and now they had arrived at an arched doorway. Wondering if it was a way out of this puzzling place, Tod lifted the iron latch and pushed the heavy door ajar. Far from being a way out however, it opened into a large walled enclosure. From where he was standing a flagged path led straight across it to another door in the opposite wall and on either side of the path neat plots of winter vegetables alternated with strips of freshly dug earth.

Apart from the walls the place looked to Tod rather like the allotments on the outskirts of the city and as soon as he was sure that there was no-one else there, he closed the door behind him and headed straight for the cabbage patch. Tugging one green globe out of the soil he stripped off its outer leaves and threw them on the ashes of an old bonfire. All the way round the enclosure trees as grey and bare as the stone were spreadeagled against the walls and after looking around him for a moment he went to sit beneath one which grew in the corner nearest to the door he'd come in by. Here, where the sun shone warmly into the angle between the walls and fired the stone with rose-gold light, it was quiet and peaceful. But outside — now close, now distant — he could still hear the voices of the children.

"Is this a school?" he asked Mim. "I thought children had to work in school."

Again Mim didn't reply and the warmth was beginning to lull Tod to sleep when he was startled by the rattle of the latch on the door on the far side of the garden. Hastily he wedged himself as deep into his corner as he could and pushed the remains of the cabbage out of sight behind the tree. The door opened and two men came through. One was short and elderly and was wearing the same kind of green overalls that Tod had already seen. The other was much younger. He was very tall and so slender that his body seemed scarcely more than a clothed skeleton. Above his blue jersey his face was pale, his hair bleached almost white. Both men moved slowly into the centre of the enclosure and stood there talking together. The tall one pointed at the ground, his hand sweeping from one plot to another. "About here..." Tod heard him say. "... need space... dangerous..." Only broken phrases of their conversation reached him and he kept very still, hoping they would soon finish and go out the way they had come in without seeing him.

At last the older man did turn and go back the way he had come but the other one strolled on into the garden. Moments later he spotted Tod. He halted, frowned and then with an exclamation left the path and strode towards his corner.

"What you doing here, son?" he asked. "No kids allowed in the kitchen garden, you know. I thought that was made clear this morning." Although he seemed displeased the man's voice was smooth, low, pleasant. "The gardeners don't like it," he said. "So it's out of bounds." He smiled, the smile warming his face, and slowly Tod stood up. "Well," said the man, "I suppose it is only the first day."

Hands in pockets he stood considering Tod for a while. Then he said, "Tell you what, since you're here you can do a little job for me... you can go back to the house and find someone — anyone — and ask them to give you a basket. Then bring it here to me. Tell them Mr. Vivian sent you — or they may think you're up to no good! Off you go now — quick as you can." With another fleeting smile he waved Tod towards the gate by which he and the gardener had entered before backing away to the path where he stood as if lost in a dream.

Increasingly bewildered by people's acceptance of his presence in this place, Tod wandered for some time along yet more intersecting pathways. He had no intention of delivering Mr. Vivian's message. The thought of going to a house where he would encounter yet more people frightened him. He wanted only to escape. But then suddenly, unexpectedly, he came upon it. It was a long, low building set well back from the path and half-buried among bushes. Constructed of the same grey stone as the garden walls, it clearly faced out the other way for on the side he could see there were neither doors nor windows. He was scurrying past it when in the distance he saw a gaggle of children come hop, skipping and jumping towards him. Cursing his bad luck he dodged out of sight among the bushes and it was as he tried to find another way out of the thicket that he came round the front of the house and saw that wherever Mr. Vivian had intended him to go, this was not it.

What Tod had found was not a house at all but an outhouse. Its one door and three windows looked out across a weedy cobbled yard to another high wall blanketed in ivy and overhung by trees. It was sheltered, secret, neglected and full of old lumber; a place where Tod saw at once he might feel safe; where he would feel at home. And indeed during the short afternoon while he first explored and then settled in it, no-one came near the building. Perhaps it too was 'out of bounds'. While daylight lasted the children's voices continued to trouble him but with darkness came silence.

At dusk when he was forced to go outside into the bushes to relieve himself it was bitterly cold. Everything sparkled with frost and his breath blew from his mouth like smoke. The air itself smelled of smoke and was sharp to breathe. He foraged in the thicket for dry leaves and twigs and brought in logs from an ancient stockpile he'd found in the yard. Then, as soon as it was dark, he lit a fire with the matches from his treasure. The fireplace was as big as a cave and now as he sat facing Mim across the leaping flames, watching the sparks dance like fireflies in the blackness of the chimney above their heads, he was warmer and more comfortable than he could ever remember being. For the first time in ages too his stomach was full. For hidden in the shadows on the other side of the room an open wooden staircase climbed to a loft where rows and rows of apples were laid out on newspaper, scenting the whole building with a sweet, cidery smell.

His shoes, their soles worn thin as paper, lay beside him, together with his bag and coat and Mim's scarf. Stretching his legs towards the warm embers, he wriggled his toes through the shreds of his socks.

'Go on with your story,' he said to Mim.

'We-ell," said Mim dreamily, "the Prince travelled on and on... until he grew so weary that it hurt to put one foot in front of the other."

"Why did he do that? Why didn't he just stop?"

"Because once he had set foot on the path, he had to go on. He had made his choice and there was no other."

"But what about the mouse? What happened to... her?"

"He took the mouse with him. He carried her in his pocket."

"Huh!" said Tod. "If his pockets were like mine he wouldn't. He couldn't!"

He thrust both hands into the pockets of his jeans and through the holes in them his fingers found his bare flesh and tickled like a mouse's feet. He heard Mim snicker and then, from somewhere inside himself, he felt a strange sensation like bubbles rising; bubbles which forced their way out through his mouth in a series of popping explosions. He could hear himself snorting, gasping, hiccupping — and listened astonished to the sound of his own laughter.

"Sheesh!" said Mim. "It isn't that funny!"

And at once Tod had a picture of his mother. Although he couldn't see her face he knew it was his mother... She was trapped in the frame of a chair whose seat had collapsed... struggling... laughing... her legs in the air, her yellow skirt frothing about her head... And he too was laughing... He was laughing and laughing until someone... someone else... said, "It isn't that funny!"

"Mim" he cried, "Mim... who...?"

The fire crackled and flared. In its guttering light the expression on Mim's tired face seemed to change from gaiety to gravity.

"Wait..." she said "Wait... Listen... It was winter... and the whole world was... was locked under ice. There was no warmth and no food anywhere. The Prince would have starved to death — except that each day the mouse found a grain or two of food which kept them alive. Then one day as they crossed a field, white with snow, the Prince saw a bird come flying and falling towards them. It was as dazzling white as the snow itself and its back was as broad as... as a bed. When it landed the bird's eyes flashed like diamonds but it could not speak to the Prince because someone had bound its beak with a steel thread..."

"Birds can't speak," said Tod grumpily.

"Well, this one could," she said, "It's storytale bird and it could." While Tod thought about this she went on with the story in a low rumble which he could barely hear and the next time he tuned in to her she was saying, "To thank the Prince for his help in freeing her beak, the bird said she would carry him out of this Frozen Land to any place he desired... So he climbed on to her soft back and she flew up, up into the air high above the clouds and snow and took him... over the hills and... far away..."

Mim stopped. Through the shifting shadows and shine of the fire, Tod saw her eyes droop and close.

"Where?" he said urgently. He threw another log on to the

fire so that the light sprang up yellow and clear with the new flames. "Where did she take him? Where did he choose?"

Mim's eyes flew open, the blue petals quivering with the shock of waking.

"Why," she said, "she took him to... she took him to The Paradise Garden of course!"

Chapter 14

Long before dawn Tod woke with the cold. The fire had gone out and the last memory of its warmth had faded from the hearth. He started to put on his coat when an idea occurred to him. Raising Mim he removed her jeans and denim jacket. Though not clean they were cleaner than his own and they were also much less threadbare — so wearing them he would look better as well as being warmer. The jacket was tight and short in the sleeves but the jeans, unrolled to their full length, were a fair fit. When he replaced Mim's jeans with his he noticed that the green velvet patch on her leg was coming away from its edges and her stuffing was showing through.

"Some in rags, some in tags and some in a velvet gown," she said reproachfully.

He decided not to take her with him. Like his worn-out clothes she might attract attention. He selected a place in one of the room's dark corners and sat her there with his bag on her lap. Then covering her with her scarf, he tilted an old wooden wheelbarrow against the wall, hiding her completely.

Outside the cold bit like a wolf. It was still dark but he was used to the dark. Tunnelling under the bushes he made his way back to the path behind the outhouse. While there was no-one else about he wanted to explore. The path led him eventually to a broad gravelled driveway and following this it wasn't long before he arrived at an oval of grass as big as a football pitch. The grass glimmered white with frost and facing him across it was a house.

So this was where Mr. Vivian had intended him to go yesterday. Tod was stunned. It seemed to him that only a Prince would dare to venture into such a place. For the pale stone walls of the house spanned the full length of the oval lawn and rose through three tiers of windows to the sky. The windows were all dark, blank as blind eyes, except in the upper row where the glass was beginning to wink red with light from the rising sun. From the driveway a double flight of steps ascended between stone balustrades to a white door under a pillared porch. Apart from two streamers of smoke rising straight into the frosty air above its roof there was no sign of life in the house.

Tod was about to creep away when footsteps crunched on the gravel behind him and a gruff voice said, "Woo! In this half light that looks like somewhere out of a fairy-tale!" Tod swung round and saw a dark-haired boy, slightly taller than himself coming across the drive towards him. "Hi!" said the boy, "You first up in your dorm?"

Tod had no idea what he meant but he nodded and at once the boy said, "Me too. I'm in West One. Where you?"

Pretending not to hear, Tod crouched down and fiddled with his shoe-lace. The boy who was dressed only in sweater and jeans, breathed on his fingers, tucked his hands under his armpits and danced about on the spot.

"I found a great swing yesterday." he said. "Takes you flying right out over a snakepit. Want to see?" And without waiting for a reply he sprang away, the gravel spurting from under his trainers as he went.

Tod didn't move, hoping the boy would give up and leave him but instead he skidded round and came galloping back.

"D'you hear those owls last night?" he said. "Spooky, eh?" He bunched his hands together, raised them to his mouth and blew through them. "Whooo... ooo" The long quavering hoot breathed out in a smoky vapour. "Come on," he urged, pummelling Tod lightly on the shoulder. "Let's go. Before all the others come out and spoil things!"

Reluctantly Tod trailed after him.

"We had a midnight feast last night," said the boy. "And Annabel caught us. She's our girl-in-charge and she's a whizzer! Didn't make any fuss. Just told us to hurry it up and leave no traces!... Is yours O.K.?"

"Yes," said Tod and the boy, yodelling loudly, dashed ahead.

Across frosted lawns, through spinneys of trees, alongside pools skinned with ice they went until they arrived at a grassy knoll. At the top stood a huge tree, black against the crimson sky. "This is it!" cried the boy, "Race you to the top!" and he bounded up the slope to grab one of the ropes that dangled from the tree's gnarled branches. Then while Tod still laboured up the bank he leapt into space and swung out over the deep hollow on the other side.

"Stupid," muttered Tod. "Swings are for babies." But he stayed there watching. Longing to try. After several more turns the boy released the rope, spat on his palms and rubbed them on his trousers.

"You scared?" he asked, looking at Tod.

"Course not," snarled Tod.

"There aren't really any snakes," said the boy. "I made that up!"

He took the rope again, ran backwards very fast and spiralled out into emptiness. Timidly Tod reached up and tugged on the second rope, feeling its strength, its roughness in his hand. From somewhere in the direction of the house a clock began to strike.

"Yippee!" yelled the boy. "Eight o'clock..." Pedalling in the air he swung himself back, dropped beside Tod and without pausing for breath ran down the bank. "Come on," he cried. "Breakfast!"

Breakfast! Drawn by the thought of food, Tod again followed him until, just as he felt he could go no further, they circled round the back of the big house and came to a gateway crowned by a clock tower. The boy charged through into a large cobbled courtyard, surrounded on all sides by stone outbuildings. The yard was crowded with children but darting skilfully between them he was one of the first to enter a doorway through which drifted the delicious smell of bacon frying. Caught up in the crowd Tod was swept along with it and minutes later he too filed into the room beyond.

Trestle tables set all the way down were rapidly filling with children and under its high rafters the room buzzed with noise. Tod had never seen so many children gathered together. Yet as they surged all round him, chattering, giggling, he had the strangest sensation that he had been somewhere like this before. The room swam before his eyes and he plumped down on to the end of the nearest bench.

He sat shaking, certain that everyone must be staring at him and that at any moment there would be an outcry. But no-one paid him the least attention. Other children joined him on the bench and none of them shrank away from him or complained that he smelled. For the first time Tod realised his smell was no longer a part of him. It had been washed out by the rain. Blown away by the wind...

Raising his head he sneaked a look around him and saw that the children in the room ranged from the very young to girls and boys who looked almost grown-up. One of these older boys, sitting at his own table, began to serve out porridge and soon a steaming bowl was place in front of Tod. Curling his fingers round it he sat for a moment warming his hands before slowly he began to eat. Still no-one said anything and after a while he relaxed enough to listen to the conversation, trying to pick up clues about where he was and what was happening here.

"No... all the girls are in The House... I mean in the house itself... Mr. Vivian thought it better..."

..."Is Maisie well enough to come to the party?"...

..."How many children from your family are here?"...

..."There's one family of six!"...

..."No... it was the youngest who won the place... But Mr. Vivian wanted whole families to be together because..."

..."He wants it to be the most amazing Christmas ever..."

Christmas! Tod looked up in astonishment. And saw that plates of egg, bacon and sausage were being passed down the table.

"Aren't families the point of it all?" asked one of the older children.

..."I suppose... but he's only got Maisie..."

..."That's the point too. He so nearly didn't..."

The talk petered out as everyone began to eat. The smell of the food tantalised Tod but he knew he shouldn't eat any more. He took one bite of the egg and then, watching the others to make sure they weren't watching him, he made a sandwich of the bacon and sausage and smuggled it into his pocket for later.

It was while he was concentrating on this that someone came running down the gangway beside him, tripped over his outstretched foot and fell against him. It was a small child. A boy with rosy cheeks and bright blue eyes. Eyes which darkened the moment they met Tod's own startled ones. Toby!

The baby set up a yell and before Tod could escape his sisters were beside him. And then, to Tod's horror, the boy who had been on the rope swings with him that morning. Crowding round his table end they stared at him with four pairs of hostile blue eyes while Toby shouted, "That's him! That's who stealed my hot doggie!"

Tod tried to lift his legs clear of the bench but the older boy blocked his way.

"Was it you?" he demanded.

"No," grunted Tod, "Wasn't me... I didn't..."

"Was!" shouted Toby "I merember..."

The older boy's mouth thinned. "Toby seems to think so," he said. "And if it was you, I'll beat you up... Bullying a baby!"

Freeing himself of the bench at last, Tod butted the boy aside, pushed between the girls and headed for the door. The girls shrieked with rage and Toby howled. The boy chased after him and seizing him by the waist of his jacket, started to drag him back. Above the growing racket Tod heard someone say, "Watch it! Here's Annabel!" and twisting in the boy's grip, he lashed out with hands and feet.

Then another voice, a light, laughing voice he'd heard before, said, "Hey-up! What's going on?... Jenny... Clare... what's the fuss about?... No fights or set-tos allowed! Not in the season of good-will and all that!... John — let him go!..."

And there was Legs, parting them all, as a swimmer parts the water, with light strokes and cuffs which meant business but did not hurt.

Chapter 15

It was early afternoon before Tod returned to the outhouse. He had just eaten a lunch of soup and sandwiches so that he was warm and comfortably full. But the outhouse was icy. Cold draughts breathed under the door and blew down the open stairway. Remembering his scarf he crawled beneath the barrow to retrieve it and found that in his absence a small, rather scrawny tortoiseshell cat had discovered Mim's soft lap and settled there. Mim's face wore a look of bland contentment.

"I love little pussy, her coat is so warm," she murmured.

For some reason both the look and her words infuriated Tod. He snatched her up by her neckerchief and pulled her out, tipping the cat off and banging his own head on the barrow as he did so. Swearing with the pain he first swiped at the cat and then ran at it, growling like a dog. The cat blinked its golden-green eyes and after a moment's dignified resistance, it fled up the stairs to the loft where it sat carefully washing its ears and whiskers as if that was what it had intended all along.

"What a naughty boy was that!" croaked Mim as he dragged her back to the inglenook and thumped her against the wall. "She never did him any harm..."

She went on muttering crossly while Tod wrapped himself in her scarf and sat tucked into the corner behind the dead fire. Voices and pictures from the morning tumbled through his head and jumbled themselves together like scraps of brightly coloured material tipped out of a rag-bag.

"What's all this?" asked Mim suddenly. "Tell!"

He opened one eye and looked at her. She was sitting tilted over from the way he'd thrown her down. Her head was awry and her hair, rucked up against the wall behind her, looked like the ruffled crest of some outlandish bird. She seemed to be squinting sideways at him with a pained and puzzled expression.

"It's a kind of a party," he said, "And all the children are here because... because they told a story..."

"Sheesh," breathed Mim. "Like me!"

"No. Not like you — you silly old bat — not that kind of a story. A real one... About their family... And if it was specially good they were invited... with their brothers and sisters... to this house — for Christmas... It's called Drake House and it belongs to Mr. Vivian... who's very rich but also very sad because his wife is dead and his daughter... Maisie... had an accident and nearly died... and so this party is for her..."

Tod stopped. He thought that he had never, ever said so much in one outpouring.

"Perhaps you were a proper chatterbox once," said Mim slily.

Tod looked at her thoughtfully. He was beginning to understand that in the lost, forgotten part of him, in the rubbed-out story of his own life, there might be surprising discoveries to be made about himself.

"Legs... Annabel... I suppose she thinks I'm here just like the others," he went on. "Because after the... the row... she made me stay with John... and Jenny and Clare... to make things... and she told us that tomorrow we all have to read our stories out... in the Library..."

"You?" said Mim softly. "Your story?"

Tod glared at her across the grey ashes.

"Stupid!" he said, "I haven't got one... I shan't go of course."

"You enjoyed this morning though," she said. "You know you did... and John was all right too!"

Tod shrugged and scowled. He fetched his bag from beneath the wheelbarrow and crammed into it the food he had saved from breakfast and lunch. He couldn't believe his good fortune and didn't believe it would continue. Sooner or later someone would say, "Who's been eating my porridge?" and he would be found out. Then what would happen? It couldn't last for ever.

"You're not staying for ever," said Mim.

Tired of her Tod turned her round with her face to the wall and then sat down again, tucking his cold hands beneath him to try and warm them. Somewhere between sleeping and waking he went back over the morning. The bare, lofty room next to the refectory. The baskets full of tangled silver tinsel. Red, green and white crepe paper. Boxes of glitter, golden foil. The shimmer of silks and sequins spilling across the tables. The children milling about the floor then sitting, talking, working. His fingers in the warmth of the room growing nimble again and learning to fashion angels and stars and baubles and bows.

"Ha!" Legs had said as she circled back to where he was sitting with John and his sisters. "I should have guessed you'd be good at this, Ted, after seeing your... after seeing Dolly..."

"Dolly!" said John, his voice coarse with scorn, "does he play with dolls!"

"No... no...," said Annabel quickly. "Of course not... but I know he once made a rather..." She had looked at Tod and Tod had looked at her and something in his look had made her stop there.

"You two know each other then?" John asked.

"Not exactly," said Annabel. "But we have met before."

"Where?" persisted John. "When?"

Annabel shook her head. "Oh... once upon a time," she said. "Just once upon a time." Then she had laughed and taken John away with her to see if Toby was all right in the Nursery. The girls had stayed with Tod. They'd giggled and squabbled and when they got in a mess with paper and glue they'd shyly asked for his help.

"Batty," he murmured now in his half sleep.

"Batty as Dracula," sniggered Mim from her corner.

When Annabel returned she'd heaped all the decorations they'd made into one of the baskets and told them to go for lunch. As the others drifted off she told Tod to wait a moment.

"What dormitory are you in, Ted?" she asked.

He'd tried his usual trick of not answering but she insisted and in desperation, remembering what John had said to him that morning, he mumbled, "Number one."

She raised her eyebrows, "You're not in West One," she said.

"No," said Tod quickly. "East One."

She gave him another odd look and then said, "O.K.... O.K....
Go for your lunch... And come to the Formal Garden at three
o'clock. I'd like you to help decorate the trees."

The Formal Garden looked like the setting for some elaborate
and mysterious game. Miniature hedgerows planted in patterns
of squares and circles and figures of eight were clipped so finely
that at first Tod thought they were carved out of green stone. Set
here and there among them, like tokens in the game, were trees
twisted and trimmed into the shapes of birds and animals. As he
wandered around them he found that the pieces of the pattern
were all linked by a labyrinth of stone pathways which led him
at last to a central circle where a fountain played. While children
swerved and skittered around him and gardeners and other adults
shouted instructions Tod simply stood and stared. He hadn't
meant to come here at all, but Mim had persuaded him. Now he
knew why. He had never seen anything so beautiful.

From the middle of the fountain a stone dragon reared into
the air. Its front claws were splayed, its head thrown back as if
to roar. Green with moss, the dragon's snaky tail coiled around
the plinth on which its hind feet rested. From its open jaws, a
great plume of water, stained scarlet by the light of the sunset,
splashed into a deep bowl. Along the rim of the bowl crouched
other smaller dragons and on their mossy backs drops of water
glittered like silver scales.

A boy of about nine rushing past Tod suddenly stopped and
came back. His black cheeks were glossy in the reflected light,
his brown eyes fizzed with excitement.

"Come and help me," he pleaded. "I can't reach high enough
to hang this up."

He waved a long paper chain under Tod"s nose and tugged
at his sleeve. Tod turned away from the fountain. Four tall
Christmas trees stood at the outer còrners of the Formal Garden.

Already they were strung with coloured lanterns and while gardeners worked at the top of them, the children were plundering the baskets of decorations which they'd made that morning and were fixing them to the lower branches.

"I'm Kevin," said the boy. "And when I grow up I'm going to be tall! Taller than you. Taller than my Dad. I'll be as tall as this tree!"

He cocked his head and peered through the branches of the tree to which he'd led Tod. An early star winked down at them.

"That's the Star of Bethlehem," he said. "Star of Wonder. Star of Light. We'll be singing about that soon. Bet I know more carols than you do!"

An hour later it was dark. The lights on the trees blazed blue, red, gold, green, violet.

All the children, standing along the paths of the Formal Garden, held candles. Somewhere, unseen, a woman strummed a guitar and swaying to its rhythms they sang carol after carol until hunger and the frost began to nip; until the candles began to gutter and smoke.

Trapped in the middle of the crowd, not knowing how to sing, Tod looked about him and saw the darkness melting at the edges. He saw the children's faces, lit from beneath by the candles and it seemed to him that the wavering flames were turning them all into images of Mim.

Still singing, the crowd began to break up and to wend its way back from the garden to the courtyard. Annabel came up beside him and took his candle stump from him.

"Supper at six," she said.

As he pushed upon the door of his outhouse, an owl squawked in the trees of the park and the gateway clock began the strokes of five. He groped his way over to the wheelbarrow corner, pulled Mim out, found his bag and set a match to the dry kindling in the hearth.

"You know where I think we are Mim," he said, standing and looking down into the shooting flames, with Mim held upright in the crook of his arm.

"Mm. Hm." she murmured.

"We're in the Paradise Garden..." said Tod. "And I want to stay here... like the Prince in your story..."

"But he didn't stay," said Mim, gazing closely into his eyes out of her own shadowy eye places.

"Why not?"

"Because the house in the garden wasn't the house with the green door," she said. "And then again — because the dragons who guarded the garden wouldn't allow it."

From nowhere the skinny cat appeared, winding itself between his legs, pushing gently at him, mewing softly. Raising his leg he heaved it off and it returned to the darkness.

"Why... not?" he repeated slowly.

"Because the Prince," said Mim with a sigh, "was not yet ready."

Chapter 16

Tod dreamed of dragons. Great winged creatures prowling the horizon, breathing out a foul, choking smoke, booming and growling by turns like thunder. He woke to find a trickle of smoke drifting across his face from the smouldering remains of the fire and the cat sitting on his feet purring and throbbing like a small engine.

He sat up coughing. The cat yawned, showing a tiny domed cavern of shell-pink skin rimmed with whiter-than-white teeth. For the first time in ages his feet felt warm and Tod didn't throw her off. Instead he ran his tongue along his own teeth and finding they felt furry and tasted nasty he wrestled out a corner of his shirt, spat on it and began to rub them vigorously. Disturbed by his movement the cat jumped off his feet, padded towards him on soft paws and rubbed her whiskery face against his. The sensation was pleasant. Nevertheless he ducked away and bared his newly polished teeth at her and told her to scram. When she ignored him and climbed on to his lap he remembered Mim's story about the Prince and the mouse, how the Prince had first ignored the mouse and later carried it with him in his pocket.

"Well, you needn't think it!" he said to the cat, but he tipped her off his lap without his usual roughness and minutes later found the remains of his first breakfast in his bag and offered it to her. She ate it greedily.

"You'll have gut ache," he said. "You'll throw up!"

The cat crouched and pricked up her ears as though she were listening. Then with a little mew she fled, not from him but from the rattling of the latch on the door as somebody outside fumbled with it. Tod had no time to consider hiding himself before the door inched open and a head appeared around it.

Annabel's head.

"Hi," she said. Then she came in and closed the door behind her.

"I've had my suspicions about you all along," she said. "At first I even wondered if you were just a figment of my imagination — I've got a pretty active imagination you know and I'm psychic too! I sense ghosts — though I've never actually seen one. So I wondered about that too. You're not a ghost, are you, Ted?"

"No," said Tod. And realised that only weeks ago he would not have been so certain.

"It was when you told me you were in Dormitory East One that I knew for sure. Because there's only West One and West Two you know. Then yesterday after supper I followed you here..." Annabel threw some twigs on to the fire so that it spluttered and flared between them. She was sitting on the floor with her long legs crossed and her elbows resting on her knees while Tod was squeezed into the corner beside Mim. She peered out into the shadowy room and then looked across at him again. "It's a good hide-away isn't it? Just the kind of place I loved to make a den in when I was a kid..." Her face thoughtful, she gazed into the fire and for some time the only sound was the dry crackle of the twigs burning.

"I'm glad you're not a ghost," she said at last. "On the other hand I could have let a ghost alone and said nothing... now I'm in a quandary, aren't I?... I mean I know you shouldn't be here... and what's more you're so... so buttoned up, Ted, that I don't know anything about you — except your name..."

Tod, who was looking not at Annabel but at Mim, saw Mim's mouth twitch, her eyebrows kink upwards.

"Actually," he said, "my name's Tod."

Mim's whole face flickered into a smile and he saw that it was right that he should lay claim to his name... to the only name he had.

"Tod," he repeated.

"Oh," said Annabel, "I see... O.K.... Tod." She edged nearer to him and leaned forward. "Come on," she urged, "tell me a bit more... I mean... I need..." But she trailed off again into silence as he shrank away from her and shook his head.

"Hey up!" she said, looking at her watch. "This'll never do. We've only got ten minutes before the Readings in the Library and I've got to make a decision. I'm an awful ditherer at the best of times... I mean my responsibility to Mr. Vivian means I ought to tell him about you but... but I feel responsible for you too... And there again perhaps it would be better for you in fact if I did tell him... I mean..."

"No," whispered Tod. "No."

He made himself look up at her. Her mouth was pursed in an expression of disapproval or uncertainty, but there was a gleam in her brown eyes she said, "It's this feeling I have... I just can't...! But listen... listen... Tod... if you promise... I mean swear that you're not about anything... well anything bad... then I'll promise to keep your secret. And I'll help you where I can... O.K.?"

She paused and then repeated, "O.K. Tod?"

He knew it was important for him to respond so he mumbled "O.K." and after only a slight hesitation Annabel said, "Right. That's a pact. And in return, you can tell me... some time... when you're ready... what your secret... *your* story you know... actually is!"

Tod looked askance at Mim. How could he ever tell Annabel a story he himself didn't know?

"I expect I'm behaving like an idiot," said Annabel, her face troubled again. "But I've decided to trust you..." She stared at him for a moment longer and then added earnestly, "You can trust me too, you know... Really!"

It was as if she suspected — guessed — that he trusted no-one. Inside Tod there seemed to be a tug-of-war going on. He wanted to say something but although he felt his lips move no sound came out and with a sigh Annabel untwined her long legs and scrambled to her feet.

"Well," she said, "if you're staying, you're going to take part. So come and listen to the others' stories."

The Library was inside The House itself. It was a high, gloomy room stacked from floor to ceiling with books which looked untouched and untouchable as though, like Tod's, their stories were locked away and inaccessible. The gloom was lightened by three tall windows which looked out on the Formal Garden and by a log fire blazing in the hearth. Above the fire two carved dragons, garlanded with leaves, writhed towards each other across the stone mantel.

Annabel placed Tod beneath one of the windows and then helped to direct other children as they came and found places to sit on the faded blue carpet. From the window beams of sunshine, spiralling with dust motes, lay across them all with a faint warmth. When everyone was settled a hush fell on the room and from a door beside the fireplace two people entered.

The first Tod recognized as Mr. Vivian. The other was a young girl he supposed must be Maisie. White, frail, thin, with long straight hair the colour of pale sand, she hovered for a moment in the doorway until her father whispered something to her and pushed her gently forward. At once she limped a few paces and sank down on the carpet amongst the other children.

Mr. Vivian stood before the fire, his hands spread wide as if to welcome them.

"Good morning, children," he said.

The dust in the shafts of sunlight seemed to thicken and spin more dizzily. Through them Tod saw not tall, slender Mr. Vivian, but a man who was short and rather fat, a man with a frizz of grey hair and a blotchy face.

Sir!

And behind him there were no leaping flames and snarling dragons among leaves, but a plain black curtain on to which white cut-out snowflakes had been pinned.

Sir... Good morning children...

School!

Like fire sweeping through dry brushwood the memories came swooping in upon Tod, engulfing him so suddenly that he gasped for air and Annabel, sitting beside him, glanced at him in concern.

"My mother left me there..." he thought... "She left me with the headmaster who held my hand and was kind but very loud... And later, in a classroom, the teacher showed me a book about a man with a yellow hat... and was surprised I could already read..."

Mr. Vivian finished speaking, words Tod had not heard, and then as the children clapped he sat down on a chair and one of the older girls stood up.

"A story about my family," she said, and began to read from a paper in her hand.

But Tod could not listen. As story followed story, and between them the children's applause rose and fell like waves, he tuned in and out of the present time in the library at Drake House. When he tuned in he heard extracts, happy, sad, funny and frightening of other people's lives. When he tuned out he was remembering events from his own.

So he recalled the day when he had been sent out of class for talking too much. He, Tod, talking too much!... And the day a dog in the school yard had nipped his ankle and he'd run home crying... to find his mother not in and Mort, angry, had sent him back... Only home had not been the shop in Old Bridge Street. So where...?

The question nagged unanswered as he listened to Kevin telling the story of how his father had met his mother... how she was a nurse and had been sent to visit an old lady who was ill... how she'd gone to the wrong house and taken the temperature of Kevin's grandmother who was 'fit as a fighting flea'... and how, when they discovered the mistake, the two women had laughed so much that Kevin's father, coming home, had fallen at once in love with the nurse 'whose laughing face shone like the midsummer sun'...

And Tod remembered the day he'd laughed with a boy called Wayne. They were painting the scenery for a play — sky and grass and trees like green lollipops — when Tod had accidentally daubed paint on Wayne's face... Wayne had shrieked and daubed paint on him too — so they had laughed and daubed until a spot of paint went into Tod's eye and he had stopped laughing and punched Wayne on the nose...

Tod shook his aching head and tried to listen as John stood up and started telling how he and his family, before Toby was born, had lived on a bus for a whole year. The bus had red-checked curtains, bunks to sleep in and a real stove which burned wood. They had travelled from the mountains to the sea and 'given lifts only to people who were not in a hurry' — because the bus was so old and slow that they called it 'The Snail'.

"Then, one day," said John, "my Grandmother died. And we had to go home..."

The words, interrupted by applause, boomed around Tod's head. Broken, distorted, insistent. Like the echo in the old railway tunnel.

"One day... mother died... had to go home... one day... mother died..."

He clutched his head in both hands, covering his ears. But the words went on clamouring and he couldn't block them out.

He began to rock where he sat, groaning as his father had on that day... on the day he'd fetched Tod home and told him... Only Mort had not groaned... He'd banged his head on the table over and over again... and bellowed and howled... And Tod, huddling in a corner too frightened to move, had wanted his mother... wanted... wanted...

And when she didn't come the emptiness of the world had gathered inside his head like darkness... And in his chest his heart had gone hard and cold and heavy as a stone...

Children moving away from him in alarm made Tod aware of the library again and of Annabel's voice cutting across the sound of his own moaning.

"It's O.K.," she was saying, "Leave him to me. It's O.K."

Looking up with hot, dry, stinging eyes, Tod saw her reach for him. With a yelp like a wounded dog he flinched away and dodging from her outstretched arms he fled through whirling blades of sunlight, down past all the windows in the room to the open door at the far end.

Chapter 17

For the rest of that day and the following night sleep eluded Tod. He tossed and turned, sometimes drifting, dozing, dreaming and sometimes wide-awake. It was as if the shock of remembering the day of his mother's death had torn aside the veils of darkness in his head because whether waking or sleeping images of his past life kept reeling through it. More pieces of the jig-saw. And they were beginning to fit together.

His mother had died in the spring-time for there were daffodils in the park when he'd walked back from school with his father... He struggled to capture a clear picture of his mother but could only achieve fleeting impressions... black hair... blue eyes... a shining blue that was dark and bright at the same time... Yes, whenever he succeeding in catching his mother with a kind of inner sideways glance, there was always brightness... and colour... A crimson skirt... A yellow jumper... Mim's yellow jumper...

From time to time throughout the strange half-life of this day, Tod was aware of the cat, prowling around him, sitting, prowling again. And of Annabel coming with food and later with blankets. He could not eat the food but she tucked the blankets round him and much later, after dark, she came and lit his fire. He was aware of her speaking to him but her voice seemed distant and indistinct until, as if she'd turned the volume up or tuned herself in properly, he heard her say, "For mercy's sake, Tod — don't die on me will you... I couldn't cope with that."

After that she went away again and he lay gazing into the flames of the fire, seeing not their scarlet and purple and gold but dull, dim faraway colours... browns, greys, greens...

The house where they'd lived had been small... redbrick... squeezed between other identical houses... a plain brown door opening straight on to the street... and at the back a yard... the space silted up with Mort's junk...

The flames fluttered wildly in a sudden draught from under the door and shadows lurking in the corners were sent flittering across the walls. In spite of the heat which had built up inside the cave of the fireplace, Tod shivered.

...During the time in that house, during his school time, Mort had not often been there... he had been 'travelling'... But afterwards... after his mother... they had left the house and gone on travelling together... he and Mort... travelling and travelling...

Uncontrollably Tod's teeth began to chatter. To stop them he ground them together until his jaws ached. Behind him he heard Mim sniffling and wriggling out of his blankets he reached for her and pulled her down beside him, holding her tight against him.

"Hush little baby — don't you cry," she wheezed.

"Shut up," said Tod, his throat tense. "I'm not crying. I never cry."

But croaking unevenly into a sorrowful little tune she repeated it, "Hush little baby, don't you cry — You know your mother was born to die-ie..."

"Shut up. Shut up. Shut up! I want to go to sleep!"

"Yes, but...," said Mim.

"Yes, but what?"

"You keep forgetting," she said, "Thursday's child has far to go..."

Releasing his hold on her, Tod pushed her away and turned his back to her.

"Not yet," he said.

"Mm. Hm!" said Mim, "That is exactly what the Prince said when the Mouse told him it was time to leave The Paradise Garden. 'Not yet. Not yet'. But the Mouse knew that the Dragons who guarded the place would not allow him to stay. It was a place where he could rest and recover from his journey but if he tried to stay..."

"What?"

"If anyone tried to stay; if they laid claim to the garden,

wanting it for ever, then the Dragons would wreak a terrible vengeance..."

Mim stopped. And Tod, sliding at last towards sleep, remembered how other stories had come to him before sleep... Stories his mother had read... Stories she'd told...

"What's more," continued Mim with a sigh, "The Prince was beginning to neglect the Mouse, forgetting how she had helped him."

"The strange thing is though," thought Tod, "I can't remember her singing to me. Not ever." He tried to picture his mother singing. But the picture wouldn't hold. He tried to hear her voice in one of the nursery songs which so haunted him. But there was only silence.

Of the rest of the long night Tod knew very little. He woke once as the grey light of dawn began to seep into the room. Feeling very hungry then, but unable to find any food left by Annabel, he crawled up the steps to the loft and took an apple. When he woke later in full light, half of it was still beside him uneaten, and Annabel was there again.

"I'm going to be in trouble over you," she said cheerfully. "I can feel it in my bones!"

Setting a plate heaped with fresh bacon sandwiches on the hearth she drove away the cat who came at once to sniff at them.

Tod, feeling greatly better, sat up.

"Hurray!" she said, sitting down on his blankets and taking one of the sandwiches herself. "I can see you're very much alive this morning — thank goodness! You make me feel like a member of the French Resistance in the war... helping to save a fugitive... or whatever..." She chewed vigorously and pushed the plate of sandwiches under Tod's nose. "You know," she said, "I've always wanted a real adventure. But now, when I seem to have got one, it's not quite what I expected and I don't know whether I'm being the brave, bold heroine who rescues the hero... or the gullible Willy Wet-Legs aiding and abetting the villain!"

Her golden brown eyes widened at him over her second sandwich.

"Are you a villain, Tod?" she asked.

Surprisingly Tod felt his face relax into a smile. Then even more surprisingly they both began to laugh. Annabel's laughter cascaded out of her in joyful ripples of sound but Tod could hear his own unfamiliar laugh as a series of short, choked-off snorts. He took another sandwich to quell it.

"Seriously though," she said. "One thing I've never been any good at is telling lies... But yesterday I had to tell some whale-sized whoppers! And I did it without so much as a blush or a stutter!"

She ran greasy fingers through her silvery-green bob of brown hair.

"They were worried about you, you know. They thought you'd had a fit or something and wanted me to take you the the nurse. But if I had, of course she'd have soon discovered... wouldn't she? And then we'd both have been in the slurry! So I told them it was John's story that did it... That it really upset you because your Gran had just died..."

The cat climbed onto her lap and she fed it a snippet of bacon rind.

"I suppose it wasn't something like that... was it?" she asked shrewdly.

Tod made a growling sound in his throat and she said, more sharply, "This torrent of information you're giving me, Tod! I can't cope with it!"

The cat turned in circles kneading her legs. She winced as its claws dug into her flesh, but instead of slapping it away as he would have done she tickled it behind its ears until it purred like a pampered tiger.

"Here am I," she said, "planning on working with children... yet I don't seem able to winkle a word out of you, let alone any hard facts. I mean simple, basic things like who are you? Where d'you come from? And what are you doing here?"

Her wide, full mouth set in a straight line and she looked sad. Wishing he could tell her something Tod turned away and glared at the cat.

"For instance," she went on. "If you've run away from home... then some body is going to be desperately worried aren't they? I mean... look at Mr. Vivian! When he thought he'd lost Maisie he was nearly demented. And then... when she came back to him... he planned this whole fabulous, fantastical party. In thanksgiving!... Because he loves her... Because she's his family... Perhaps you should think about that..."

Tod tried very hard to imagine Mort loving him enough to want to celebrate his return. Failing miserably he shook his head. "No," he said. "There isn't... there's no..."

"I see," said Annabel. "You mean... you've no family..."

She tipped dregs of water out of his mug on to the ashes of the fire, took a flask from her bag and poured him a cup of cocoa. While Tod sipped the hot drink she went on talking and he began to see that she was inventing possibilities for him, constructing stories that would explain him and all he had to do was to agree with bits here and there in order to satisfy her that she was on the right lines.

So, gradually, Annabel was led by her own imagination and his cunningly place 'yesses' and 'noes' into believing that he had absconded from a children's home, hitch-hiked to this party which he'd learned about from a friend, and was on his way to find another friend, an older boy who'd once been in the same 'home' with him...

"That's all very well," she said. "But what if when you get there this boy doesn't really want you... or can't... you know...? What will you do then?"

Beside him, Mim, lying with her face pressed into his thigh, whispered, "What will Poor Robin do then, poor thing?" and giggled. Tod put his hand on her head and rammed it tighter against him.

"What's the boy's name?" continued Annabel, feeding the cat with the last left-over bacon rind.

"Robin," said Tod promptly. Beneath his hand he could feel Mim twitching and shaking.

"And where does he live?" asked Annabel. "I mean unless

you know where you're going..."

Tod stalled. He knew no names of places. Not even the name of the place where he was now.

"I think you ought to tell me." she persisted.

"I forget what it's called." he said "But it's a big town not far from here."

Annabel tried a name. He shook his head. She tried another and he at once nodded as if that was it. As if all it had needed was a jolt to his memory. But Annabel looked doubtful.

"That's still a long way off," she said "And in winter! And you shouldn't hitch-hike you know. You really shouldn't! All kinds of... of horrible things could happen..."

Then, with one of the swift changes of direction she was prone to, she told him that in a week's time, on New Year's Eve, there was going to be a 'Big Surprise Finale' to the party and that on the following day, everyone would be going home.

"You can't stay after that," she said, "because The House is going to be closed down. Mr. Vivian is taking Maisie abroad... to the sun..."

She lifted the cat from her knee, set it on its feet and stood up. "If I were going home myself," she said, "I think I'd... but I'm not... I'm going to stay with a friend who should have been here with me... except she fell prey to some kind of mystery bug..." She shook the crumbs from her short skirt and laughed. "Bit like me really, I suppose," she said, "Only my mystery bug waited until I got here. And came in the shape of a boy!"

Crossing over to Tod she prodded him gently with her toe and made him look up at her. "What's... what's this boy — Robin's — address?" she said. "The place he lives in is... well it's a city... enormous... anonymous..."

A shadow on her face, an edge in her voice suggested to Tod that after all she doubted the story they'd concocted. He looked down, his mind a blank. Under his hand he could feel the warmth of Mim and sensed she was trying to say something. He leaned over her and just within his hearing she murmured four words. As he repeated them aloud for Annabel he knew

that 'All Saints Terrace' had been the name of the street where
he'd live with his mother and father and that 'Five' was the number
of the house with the yard full of junk.

"Ha!" said Annabel. But she didn't question him any further.
Instead she went and peered out of the cobwebby window,
blinking into the dazzle of sunshine.

"All the children," she said, "are hoping it will snow before
tomorrow. Fat chance I guess. There isn't a cloud in the sky!"

Then, with a quick word to Tod that she'd fetch him later
and show him where he could have a shower and spruce himself
up for Christmas Day, she departed.

Chapter 18

Christmas Day passed in a whirl of balloons and crackers, streamers and paper hats. Tod forgot his usual restraint, ate too much turkey, and felt ill.

It did not snow. Not for Christmas Day, nor later. The sky stayed a cold, clean blue and the sun shone. Because of the continuing fine weather the children were more often out of doors than in. Occasionally, when cornered by Kevin or Jenny, Tod would be drawn into one of their games. But most of the time he wandered the grounds by himself and the others, deciding he was a loner, an oddity, paid him little attention.

The days slid by as though he were entranced; held in a state where all that he did in the present was merely a hazy background to his returning memories of the past. Mostly these memories were of school and the house in All Saint's Terrace. But he also remembered the time when, alone with his father, the two of them became wanderers, moving from city to city, from lodging to lodging until they settled at last in the condemned tenement between Rivermarsh and Old Bridge Streets. These memories he thrust away, not wanting to examine them.

Throughout this time he spent very little time with Mim who sat abandoned in her chimney corner, gathering a grey coating of dust and ashes, looking more and more dejected. Then the weather began to change. The weather-cock on the clock tower creaked slowly round and the wind started to blow, sighing in cold gusts from the north. A thin film of cloud glazed the eye of the sun one day and by the next had thickened to cover the whole sky, taking on a murky yellowish tinge like the colour of an old bruise. In the distance the Dream Land hills turned a lowering slatey-blue and then vanished in the cloud.

By noon of this day the children had retreated indoors and

Tod went back to his out-house which was cold now and comfortless. As soon as he entered he could hear a faint crooning coming from Mim's corner and after a while he picked up the words which were mumbling along with the tune.

"The North wind doth blow and we shall have snow — and what will the robin do then poor thing?" sang Mim. "He'll hide in a barn and keep himself warm — and tuck his head under his wing — poor thing!'

In the sallow, oppressive light, her eyes were like empty hollows.

"Listen," she pleaded. "Listen to the story of the Prince and the dragons..."

Snatching up her black scarf Tod threw it over her head. Then he went out again.

In the Library there was a Punch and Judy show. Huddled round the blazing fire, the children watched quietly. There was something subdued, even forlorn, in the atmosphere. Tod could see Annabel sitting with John and Clare and Jenny on the other side of the room. Toby was on her knee. She looked up as he came in, but made no sign to suggest he should join them. A sudden rage filled him, flaring in his chest as though his stone, so shrunken, so little noticed lately, had exploded into flames. He thumped down on the carpet, driving his bony elbow hard into the arm of the girl beside him. When she looked up, outraged, her mouth already shaped to cry, he bared his teeth at her so that she was frightened into silence, merely rubbing the sore place over and over again, while tears splodged on to her skirt. The flames in Tod's chest died down but another different heat spread up his neck and into his face. He felt wretched. He did not enjoy the show. He couldn't anyway have laughed at Mr. Punch who reminded him forcibly of Mort. Before it ended, he crept out again.

In the Formal Garden the tree decorations looked tarnished and bedraggled. The first feathery flakes of snow were twisting down out of the bleak sky and as he dawdled across the lawn he caught them cold and stinging on his tongue. On the fringes of the park two gardeners were sawing a fallen tree, cutting it into pale golden chunks and stacking them neatly in a trailer behind a Landrover. They looked up as he idled past.

"You're going to get your snow then — after all!" said one of them.

"Is that wood for the fire?" enquired Tod, nodding towards the trailer. The gardeners didn't answer but turned away and began to pack up their tools. While they had their backs to him, Tod sneaked a couple of logs and pushed them under his coat. Then he walked rapidly back towards the house.

The snow was now whirligigging down, thickening and darkening the air, beginning to whiten the grass. The sky seemed to have lowered itself on to the tree-tops and was as grey as the pelt of a wolf. When he reached the oval lawn again, Tod found children running in all directions, yelling with excitement. Like a small clown Toby came waddling towards him, his podgy hands clasping and unclasping as he tried to catch some of the swarming snowflakes. Chortling with delight he flung his arms around Tod's leg and clung there, shouting, "Bumble-emma... bumble-emma... Need a bumble-emma!"

Nervously, awkwardly, Tod detached him.

"What?" he said.

"Yes!" crowed Toby, "Wet! Need a bumble-emma!"

"He means an umbrella," giggled Jenny, materialising out of the blizzard. "That's his word for umbrella." And taking Toby's hand she tugged him away, disappearing into the snow again just as Annabel loomed out of it.

"Inside!" yelled Annabel, waving her arms. "All of you! At once!" Noticing Tod she stopped and said, "Hey up, Tod, you should go in too." She swung round to flap at a group of older boys who were haring across the lawns. "You can come out later when it stops," she cried. But the boys raced on, ignoring her.

"Oh well!" she said, "I suppose it'll cheer them up. A lot of them were getting very homesick..."

The snow however went on and on and no-one came out later. When Tod returned from the refectory after supper it clustered thickly on his eyelashes and smudged out his footsteps even as he made them. Long after that, when Annabel came across to the outhouse, she said it was still falling — only more slowly. And the sky was clearing.

Her hair and her anorak were flecked with snow. In her hand she carried a pair of shoes and slung across her back was her big shoulder bag.

"Can't stop long, Hot Toddy," she said. And laughed. Tod, sitting with his feet almost in the smouldering cinders of his log fire, realised his face was burning and he must look as hot as he felt.

"Lots of the little ones are fizzing like firecrackers," she said, wiping a drop off the end of her nose with her sleeve. "What with the snow... and tomorrow and everything... I shall have to get back to help..."

She dropped the shoes and began to rummage in her bag, flicking things out of it just as she had the first time Tod met her.

"Here," she said. "This is for you... I might not have time to see you tomorrow and I wanted... well you can see..."

She thrust towards him a brown paper packet which fell open as soon as he touched it. Inside it were sandwiches, crisps, biscuits, fruit — and slipping out of the folds of the paper, an envelope on which she had written her own name and an address.

"I've made up my mind how to do it," she said. "So that I shan't be scrunched up with worry about you... I don't want to find myself on T.V. you know! Not that way anyway! Being the last person to see you alive... and having to explain why I didn't say anything..."

She rambled on. And Tod, with a lurching, breathless sensation, discovered that inside the envelope there were two five pound notes.

"Just... just to help..." she said, seeming shy all at once, "and don't say no because I won't listen... I wish it was more... Anyway you'll have to buy postcards — and stamps."

Pushing off the cat which was curled up on his knees, Tod stood up.

"What for?" he asked. Even to him it sounded abrupt and ungracious but Annabel didn't seem to notice. She picked up the shoes and placed them in the hearthplace. "Those too," she said "I don't need them and yours are as full of holes as a collander. They won't keep your toes in soon... let alone the cold out..."

Tod felt very uncomfortable. Backing away he shook his head and misunderstanding him, she said, "Don't be daft, Tod... they could easily be boy's shoes... look at them — the clumpy great clogs... But if you wear extra socks they'll probably fit..." Without giving him time to argue she said, "As for the post-cards, I want you to send them about once a week until you arrive at your friend's house... then I'll relax... No need to write anything... Just a card and your name... O.K.?"

She stepped towards him and put her hands on his shoulders.

"Good Luck, Tod!" she said.

Rigid under her touch, he stammered and shuffled and finally pulled away. Annabel's face flickered with changing and contradictory expressions. Hurt, perplexed, amused, exasperated. Suddenly Tod wanted desperately to tell her the truth about himself but the necessary words would not come. Instead he heard his own voice asking her gruffly if she was going back in the aeroplane.

"Ha!" she said. "No. I'm not going home remember? Anyway Nick — the pilot — couldn't take me. He's otherwise engaged! I'm going by train." She moved back to the door. "Heigh-ho," she said. "Must go!" She opened it cautiously, letting in a flurry of snow. "Enjoy the high-jinks tomorrow!" From outside she put her head back round the door. "See you some time," she said. And left the words hanging in the air like a question as she banged the door behind her.

Tod returned to the fire and threw himself down among the blankets, burying his head in their grey warmth. The cat sniffed at his hair and then stole away into the shadows. From her corner Mim started first to zizz and then to sing,

"O, what pain it is to part. Can I leave thee, can I leave thee?

O, what pain it is to part!"

Tod covered his ears and hummed loudly to block out the sound. Dimly, through the droning, he was aware that Mim had stopped singing and was trying once more to tell him her story.

Chapter 19

New Year's Eve dawned fine and clear. Over the park the snow lay as crisp and smooth as an unbroken crust. The intense white light beating back from it was the same as the light from the sky so that trees and bushes and buildings were evenly lit and shadowless. Everything was starkly black and white and grey. It was as though all the life had drained out of Drake House and its gardens.

In the outhouse, beside the dead fire, Tod packed up his few belongings and stacked them beside Mim. Several times since he woke she had begun the story of the Prince and the dragons in the Paradise Garden, but Tod had sullenly refused to listen and eventually she gave up. Her head hung slackly where the stuffing had become limp and on an impulse Tod picked her up, dusted her down and tightened the fraying rag of her neckerchief so that it held her head upright again. Then he smoothed her sooty hair and sat her on top of his things.

Through all this time she kept her eyes fixed on him but said nothing.

"Tomorrow morning," said Tod. "That's when we'll go. Like all the others. Tonight I want to see the farewell celebrations." She did not respond to this either and suddenly angry he stuck out his tongue at her and left the building.

Tod did not see Annabel all day. At supper time in the refectory there was no food, only hot drinks. One of the older women told the children that they were to wait where they were and soon they would be fetched. In a buzz of impatient noise, over-hot in their coats, they sat and fidgeted.

The woman fetched two baskets and set them on the table beside Tod. Then she summoned together a group of older boys and handing them the baskets she whispered something to them which made them grin and jig about, before they streamed away down the aisles and through the door into the courtyard.

"Bring at least fifty!" she bawled after them. "And make sure they're all good!"

At last Annabel appeared. She paid no attention to the children but spoke to the woman in charge. At once, as if this was the signal they'd been waiting for, the helpers began to gather the children together. Tod hung back on the fringe of the crowd, unwilling to be trapped within it but wanting to go with them wherever they were going.

Underfoot the snow was already softening, turning to slush. The sharp, dry cold of the last fortnight had gone and the night air felt muggy, almost warm. It smelled strongly of woodsmoke. Within minutes Tod realised that the chattering file of children was being led towards the forbidden garden where he had first encountered Mr. Vivian.

Well before they reached the arched entrance they could see plumes of grey smoke feathering out above the high wall. The smoke spread and eddied, its fuzzy edges stained red, vermilion, rose. And as the children drew closer to the hidden garden they could hear a long, steady roaring punctuated by snapping, snarling sounds. A quiver of excitement passed through the file and John who was right behind Tod shouted,

"Hoo! Listen to that kids!... 'Ere be dragons!"

The words struck Tod like a blow. He thought of Mim's untold story and a cold shiver crawled up his neck and under his hair. John started slashing about him with an imaginary sword scattering the nearest children who giggled and joined in the game. Then the crowd pushed forward, jostling towards the gate. Tod hesitated, held back. But he was swept along with the others as they surged through the arch and into the garden.

Inside the walls the snow had melted entirely leaving the bare, black earth exposed. And instead of the neat plots of winter vegetables he had seen on his first day, there was an enormous pyramid of wood blazing at the centre of the garden.

"A bonfire!" shrieked the children fanning out to surround

it. "A bonfire!"

As those coming in behind pressed forward Tod was carried right against the rope which encircled the fire. The stone in his chest was jumping like a live thing and he put his hand over it to quieten it. From the base of the pyramid fiery eyes seemed to wink and glare at him out of every crevice while the flames licked up through the logs with greedy crimson tongues before springing into the dark sky as if to devour it too. He moved back from the ferocious heat and Kevin came dancing into the space beside him.

"Look," he shouted, "Look!"

He was pointing to another roped off area beneath the wall where gardeners were moving to and fro, stopping, stooping, moving again. But before Tod could make sense of what they were doing, Kevin dashed away crying, "Whee! Fireworks! I'm good at fireworks! My Dad always let's me..." His voice trailed off as he disappeared into the crowd and then, filling the garden with more sound and fury, the display began.

Fireworks whizzed and whirred and whirled. Rockets fizzed yellow against the blackness of the sky. Flares of green, white and purple fire fountained from the blackness of the earth. Showers of sparks splashed all over the garden and on to the upturned faces of the children. Everything banged or whooshed, whistled or screamed.

Tod was dazzled and deafened. In his confusion a phrase of Mim's kept repeating itself inside his head... "The Dragons wouldn't allow... they wouldn't allow him to stay..." He couldn't stay. He shouldn't have tried to stay. Turning from the fire he tried to worm his way through the densely packed crowd, back to the gate. But blocking his escape even as he reached it, came a slow procession of adults. They were carrying bowls and baskets, dishes and platters all piled high with food; glossy brown sausages and glistening hunks of crisp roast chicken; baked potatoes oozing with butter; savoury burgers and crusty buns; spicy warm ginger-bread, hot jammy doughnuts and shining golden toffee apples.

Hungry, knowing this would be his last good meal for a long time, Tod turned back. As he did so, beyond the din in the garden, he thought he heard a low mutter of thunder threatening from the faraway horizon of the hills.

Later, much later, when all except a few of the older children had dispersed to their dormitories, Tod crept back to his room. A few, fat drops of rain fell out of the sky, cooling his hot face. Putting his shoulder to the door of the outhouse he pushed hard and then staggered as, unlatched, it flew open under his weight. Wearily he crossed the flagstones to the fire place and blinking with tiredness, he put out his hand to lift Mim off his things.

And found she was not there.

His bag, her scarf, Annabel's blankets, they were all there, just as he had left them. But Mim, so patiently waiting for his return, had gone.

He searched and searched, looking everywhere, tumbling the assorted lumber of the outhouse in all directions as he peered under, over and behind it. In his desperation he behaved as though Mim might have sneaked away and hidden herself to tease or punish him.

The cat, alarmed by his violent action, disappeared into the loft. And it was when he followed her there that he began to understand what might have happened. For in his absence the loft had been invaded. The dust was printed with footmarks. Fruit was scattered over the floor, the paper beneath it trampled and torn. And most of the apples had gone.

In a rapid succession of pictures Tod saw the woman in the refectory, the boys with their baskets, the raided loft, the toffee apples round the bonfire...

The bonfire... boys... and Mim missing... He did not need pictures to take him any further. With a howl he set off into the night again.

The distant grumblings from the horizon had gathered themselves together and were now rumbling with loud menace over his head. And as though in angry answer to the flares from the garden, lines of blinding light were being scribbled across the darkness.

"Dragons," whispered Mim's voice in his head "Listen. The dragons..."

Groaning Tod plunged through the gate in the walled garden and saw, as in a nightmare, what he had most feared to see.

The fire, much smaller but still fiercely glowing, hissed and spat as the rain, now beginning to fall in earnest, sizzled into it. Against its blood-red light six or seven prancing figures were silhouetted. They were inside the rope, dancing in a circle, and around their feet, the powdery ash rose and drifted like fresh smoke. And as they danced they whooped and chanted, war-cry and words intertwined.

"Hiya! Hi-ya! Hi-ya!

We found a guy-ya, guy-ya, guy-ya!

Hi-ya! Hi-ya! We found a guy!"

"No!" shouted Tod, "No! Stop!"

For brandished high above the tallest boy's head, flopping and flapping like a rag-doll as he bounced up and down, was Mim.

Through the noise they were making the children did not hear him. But Tod could hear Mim. Across the beat of their incantation and the stamp of their feet, he could hear the frail, husky mew of her voice as she cried to him for help.

As he dived under the rope the boy who held her slowed down and retracted his arm. Mim jerked back and Tod saw her eyes, wide and terrified.

"No-o!" he yelled.

Head down, arms flailing, he hurtled into the circle of children. His head thudded into the boy's midriff and he reeled back, his neck wracked with pain. Retching and gasping the other boy doubled up and Mim flew from his grasp. She flumped down into the smoking embers and squealed as the flames, fanned into new life by her fall, reached out for her. The other children skidded to a shocked halt and in that brief pause Tod snatched Mim up by the hair scorching his hand in the flames. Then as the others revived and darted forward to catch him, he zig-zagged between them, hurdled the rope and raced for the far gate.

As he ran he banged and buffeted Mim to put out the little lines of fire that were nibbling into her trousers while she wheezed and croaked in protest.

Still running, sounds of pursuit behind him, he reached the outhouse. Grabbing his things from the hearth he bundled Mim in her scarf and held her tight in his arms. Then, by hidden paths, he headed out into the park where the children's voices finally faded away and where the full force of the storm broke over him.

There, for the first time since his mother died, Tod started to cry.

He wept and sobbed and wailed as though all the unshed tears of his childhood were being released in one outpouring. The tears which flooded down his cheeks mingled with the falling rain and streamed over Mim's black hair, washing it clean of all the dust and ashes of the fires in the Paradise Garden.

PART FOUR

Tod

Chapter 20

Tod was many miles from Drake House when he sent his first postcard to Annabel. It was a blurry picture of a village street with grey stone houses and a church at the end. On the back he wrote, "Yor shoos are good. Im alrite, Tod."

The handwriting was clumsy, childish, but for the rest of that day he turned the words over in his mind, marvelling that he, Tod, had written them.

His travels had resumed their old pattern except that he had taken to walking by day and sleeping by night. During these unseasonably mild days he was alternately drenched by heavy showers and dried by a harshly brilliant sun. He was heading once more for the hills. Though still distant, they stayed clearly visible now and sometimes when the sun shone a rainbow would arch between them and the plain where he walked. When the rain sluiced over him he cursed it but without rancour. His burned hand had healed. He ate well enough. The sensation of the stone in his chest was little more now than a shadow. There was a new strength in him.

One day, trudging along a narrow lane between high banks, he was caught in the full glare of the setting sun as its beams struck through the bars of a field gate. He stopped to enjoy its warmth and looking down, saw himself highlighted by its brightness. There was a sizeable gap between his jeans and his socks. His tacked up dufflecoat scarcely reached to his knees. Everything was tight, threadbare, fraying, falling apart. With a catch of laughter in his throat he raised his arms and stood posed like a scarecrow.

"Hey, Mim!" he said, "Here is the Man all tattered and torn!"

"And here," croaked Mim, "is the Maiden all forlorn!"

It was the first time she had spoken in two days. Since

leaving The Paradise Garden the balance between them had altered. Tod talked more, Mim less. She rarely sang and could not be drawn into telling him any more of the Prince's story. At first he thought this was because she was upset over his refusal to listen to her story of the dragons, a refusal which had so nearly brought disaster on them both. Later however he realised it was because she was too weary.

The constant soakings kept turning her stuffing to a soggy pulp and each time it dried out it lost some of its bulk. So she had grown thin and frail. Her trousers were charred, her legs scarred from her tumble into the fire. The wool of her jumper was felted and its once bright mimosa yellow was now paler than primrose. Worst of all, her face, grimed by soot and bleached by the sun, had greyed to the colour of bone. Only her flower eyes kept a memory of their original blue.

"Mm. Hm," she murmured, interrupting his thoughts as she had so often done, "All I am made of — only trash is — and soon, soon — will be dust and ashes!"

"Don't," whispered Tod. For a moment he felt again the hard weight of his stone. "Don't talk rubbish!" he said loudly.

"You mean trash!" she giggled, with a touch of her old humour.

With the sun gone the dusk advanced fast. It was time he found somewhere to settle and sleep. A road sign on his right gave him the name of the village whose lights he could already see. To his left there was a stile and beside it a finger post pointed across a heathy wilderness. 'The Common' it said. Tod decided on the stile.

"I wish you'd tell me the rest of the Prince's story," he said to Mim as he climbed over it. "Surely there is some more. Surely it has an ending".

Behind him he thought he heard her sigh, "Sheesh", but the faint sound was lost as another squall of rain spat at them out of the darkness. The rain was washing Mim out, he thought, taking all shape and colour from her. She was like the stories in his book whose pencilled words were fading into invisibility on the page. He, on the other hand, was like a picture in a magic painting book whose shapes and colours begin to appear only when they are brushed with water. Daily more and more of himself was coming into view. And the picture which was emerging was not so terrible after all. His memories told him that he had not always been his father's 'dirty thief', silent, sullen, hating and hateful. Nor had he always been a 'no-name'. His name was still lost but he knew he must once have had one. Because he had been to school, had friends, talked, laughed... and although he had lost his temper often and got into trouble sometimes his mother had not found him ugly and vicious. She had loved him...

For several minutes Tod had been climbing, treading through wiry heather and bilberry bushes but now his feet began to speed up on a grassy downward slope. The rain had eased off and as the moon, almost full, slid from behind the clouds he saw he was on the rim of a shallow hollow filled with bracken and gorse. And where the hollow bottomed out there was a cluster of stunted evergreen trees.

"Looks good," he said to Mim.

He began to work his way down it, squeezing carefully between the clumps of scratchy gorse until he reached the trees. With both hands he parted the low hanging branches, swearing as more cold water sprayed all over him. Easing himself under them he felt his way forward.

At first he could see nothing. His feet crackled over hard, dry leaves. Sharp twigs clawed at his hands and face. Head and shoulders struck against low branches. Then, as the whole thicket rustled and creaked in a gust of wind and moonlight spilled between the shifting leaves, he saw, spread in the centre of the hollow as if prepared and waiting for him, an old mattress. He had just enough time to take in the rusty springs poking through its striped cover, the stained pillow, the rolled up sleeping bag, when the moonlight went.

Before his eyes could re-adjust to the darkness, there was a slight rasping sound and less than an arm's length away he saw the flicker of a matchflame. And in the same instant, just above his head, he saw pinpoints of its reflected light glinting at him out of two round black eyes. As Tod recoiled in alarm the eyes dipped towards him. And around them the wavering matchlight played over the wildly scrambled hair of a monstrous shaggy head.

With a shriek Tod thrust himself backwards among the trees. The light guttered out and he could hear Mim whimpering as he forced his body through the resisting branches and they were snared, released, and snared again. As well as the racket they were making there was a snarling, growling sound as of a huge and angry animal and he had the sense of something groping towards him, feeling for him in the thick dark.

He had almost given up hope of escaping from the mesh of branches when he broke through into the open air and feet heavy with fear, started to scramble up the bank. Behind him there were crashing, trampling noises as the creature in the thicket barged through after him but when he reached the crest of the hollow there was silence. He glanced over his shoulder and at that moment the moon rode out again. Outlined in its silver light, he saw the massive figure of a man, lion-headed, taller than the trees. The man had stayed at the foot of the slope and stood there, motionless, except that as Tod watched he slowly raised one arm and shook his fist at the sky.

"That's right," bawled a gruff, strong voice. "Run and hide yourself! Hide your face from the unsightly poor... the dispossessed..."

Dropping on to hands and knees Tod began to crawl in the direction of the road. From the hollow the voice continued to cry, like a wolf baying at the moon.

"Run from the homeless... the outcast... the everlasting wanderer... For it is written... the Son of Man hath not any place to lay his head..."

The voice pursued him but the man did not. Through the watery days which followed, however, Tod was haunted by the tramp's words. He stopped thinking of the past and began for the first time to consider the future.

"Where am I going?" he asked Mim. "Where *am* I going?"

And when she didn't reply, he said, "I'm not going anywhere. There isn't anywhere for me to go! I'm just like him... I'm an outcast... I shall have to go on wandering for the rest of my life..."

He felt hollow with the horror of it and unable to continue walking he sat down on a stone and said, "Tell me the story of the Prince, Mim. What happened to him? Where did *he* go?"

She rustled at his back and faintly, very faintly, he heard her say

"Remember... The House... with the Green Door."

He shook his head. He could not remember. Except for that one brief glimpse that he'd had of the door itself, it seemed to belong to a part of his life that was still hidden, inaccessible. It was as if there was a barrier there, a wall of dark glass beyond which he could not go. And when he tried to peer through it he was baffled, tantalised by shadows. It was like trying to recall an unremembered dream.

"If only there was somebody who could tell me," he said, scuffing Annabel's shoes in the dust and wishing suddenly that she herself was there.

"Somebody," murmured Mim. "Somebody came..."

She stopped and gave a little mew of exasperation as though those were not the words she had meant to say. Or had forgotten what came next. Then the sun, swallowed into the belly of a cloud five minutes earlier, shot out again. Under its glare the grass grew instantly greener and another rainbow sprang up from somewhere in a far cleft of the hills.

"No," said Mim, "there's nobody."

But as if the sun had revived her too, she began to zizz, repeating her last word over and over.

"Nobody... nobody... nobody..." she droned. "Nobody... nobody... told me..."

"What nobody, nobody knows," chanted Tod, the words rising unexpectedly and bursting like bubbles against the rim of his memory.

"Yes," gasped Mim, "Yes... yes... yes..."

"But now I know," he continued slowly, "where the rainbow ends.."

"Yes," said Mim again. "Yes!"

Tod stared across the fields to the place where the rainbow seemed to end. Then shrugging Mim higher on to his shoulders he stood up and repeating the words like a spell he began once more to plod through the puddles along the road.

Chapter 21

" Still O.K. haven't hitchhieked once. Not far to go now. Tod."
The postcard, with its over-bright view of the hills, slid between the stiff lips of the letter box and with a grunt of satisfaction Tod turned away. It was his second card to Annabel. And in his bones, along his blood, he felt the amazing truth of its message. He had not far to go.

He was hungry again. He was dirty. He was weary and footsore. But none of these things mattered. For without being able to say how — or why — he knew where he was.

Each day for the past three days as he had drawn closer and closer to the hills the sense of their familiarity had grown steadily stronger. Now, as he turned his back on the post-box and set off along the road which wound towards them, they were very close. Knobbed with outcrops of rock, lined with gullies, their hunched shapes against the pale forget-me-not blue of the sky were like the half-remembered faces of people known long ago. He began to know in advance what he would see at each bend on the road. And beyond the hills, lay the sea. He could not see it, but he knew it was there. Moreover he could smell it, sharp and salty on the strong gusts of wind which brought the still frequent showers. It was like coming to a place visited time and again in a dream; a place that was utterly strange yet completely familiar.

The bewildering sense he had of both knowing and not knowing where he was filled Tod with an almost unbearable excitement. For the first time he saw how beautiful the world was. And its beauty made him want to shout, laugh, stamp, sing, cry. Strangest of all, these sensations seemed to spring, full of life, from the very place where once his stone had lain with a dead and dreadful weight.

Ahead of him, marking another twist in the road, stood a single tall Scots pine. Tod's footsteps quickened. He hopped and skipped, kicked pebbles into the hedge, beat the air with his hands as though he were conducting a band to whose cheerful rhythms he was marching.

The pine tree swayed and sighed as the wind skirled around it. Then huffing on down the road the breeze dragged rough fingers through Tod's tangled curls and on his shoulder he felt Mim's head lift.

"Tired," she whispered. "So tired... Tod."

He rubbed his cheek against her hair which was matted now to a bedraggled, shineless mop.

"Soon be there," he said.

She gave a weak little giggle.

"Where... where... soon be there... where... where..." she repeated.

Her voice, almost inaudible these days, trailed away altogether as a car, grinding into low gear for the corner, swerved past them. Tod's empty stomach seemed to turn right over. Three... two... one pace and he would see, would surely see...

"The river," husked Mim, nodding against his neck, "the tide in the river..."

And there indeed it was. In all its shining glory. As Tod reached the tree he could see it, no more than half a mile away. Not quite as wide as he remembered it but stretching as he had known it would, to the very foot of the hills.

Tod sat on a bollard on the quayside. Behind him a row of small cottages built of the same grey stone as the quay looked closed up and uninhabited. No smoke puffed out of their chimneys. Wooden shutters, their blue paint faded and flaking, were firmly fastened across their windows.

Apart from him the quay was deserted.

Below him water sucked and slapped at the stone jetty. The waves, pearl and silver when the light fell on them, had dulled to pewter as heavy clouds moving inland from the unseen sea had again covered the sun.

Way out in midstream he could see the ferry boat like a slow black beetle, crawling its way over to the farther side.

He had no money for the crossing.

Twenty four hours ago he had spent the last of Annabel's money on food and now he was stranded. The ferryman, scrawny from a long lifetime of hard work, tawny from exposure to all weathers, had looked at him with hostile, sea-blue eyes.

"No free lifts." he said. "What d'you take me for — a charitable institution? This is my livelihood, mate!"

"But I must..." said Tod..."I have to get across."

"Then you have to get a pound first," said the man. "You can't kid me you're only half-fare either..."

Grumbling and growling at the paid-up passengers who scarcely half-filled the boat, he had cast off and left Tod there.

Cold and dejected, Tod sat and squinted through the smoke-grey light trying to see when the boat would enter the creek which ran into the narrow gap between two rocky outcrops of the hills; trying to judge how long it would be before it returned.

It was long past noon and he guessed that the ferry's journeys would end before night fall. His only hope was that if any passengers turned up for the final crossing, there would be someone from whom he could beg his fare.

To while away the time he began to go through the things in his fisherman's bag, wondering if there was anything at all among his treasures that he could barter for a pound. He reminded himself of Annabel as his fingers, pushing the small collection around and around the inside of the bag, raked up his book of stories and sent it flapping on to the stones of the quay. He picked it up and flicked the pages over. They were brown and stained along the edges where water had got into them and the pencil marks were now so worn away that they were unreadable.

"Look," he said to Mim, holding it up in front of her face. "Useless!" and he rammed it back in his bag.

"Never mind," said Mim with surprising strength, "I know

the story of the Prince by heart."

"Well, why don't you finish it then?" said Tod surlily. "A story without an ending is no good at all."

Mim sighed. He felt the cool breath waft gently against his ear. Across the river, in the shadow cast by the hill, he saw the water whiten around the prow of the ferry boat as it swung out of the creek and into the main stream again.

"There are endings and endings," she said dreamily. "Some are sad and the others are really beginnings in disguise."

Tod sniffed.

"Which sort is this?" he asked.

"Both," said Mim softly.

A shaft of light striking between the ragged clouds lit up the boat for an instant where it wallowed in midstream.

"Go on," urged Tod.

"Well," murmured Mim. "After... long after... the Prince escaped the dragons, he came to a pool of water so wide that he couldn't see across to the other side..."

"Was there a boat?"

"No boat. No way across at all. He thought his journey had come to an end before he had found what he came to seek and so he sat sadly on the shore and watched the waves run in and out..."

"What about the Mouse?"

"Mm. Hm," said Mim after a pause. "The Mouse had done all she could... there was nothing more... and all she wanted was rest..."

"I reckon that's what the Prince wanted too," said Tod.

"No," said Mim. "No."

Behind them Tod heard footsteps and voices as a group of people came down the path alongside the cottages and then stood chatting on the quay. The boat now was clearly visible. In the bows the ferryman's yellow sou'wester stood out against the sullen greys of water and sky as rain began to sweep in long slanting lines out of the clouds.

"As the Prince watched the waves his eye caught sight of

something glinting gold which rolled in and out among them and moving forward he reached down into the surf to pluck it out. When he saw what it was, he started back in surprise for it was a beautiful fish with gleaming scales as golden as the sun and yellow eyes as round as the moon. And it was snared by the tail in a shred of fisherman's net."

Mim's voice ran on steadily, stronger than it had been for weeks, and Tod listened hard, oblivious of all that was going on around him.

"The Prince tried once to release the fish but the waves snatched it away before it was free. He tried a second time but the fish's own struggles took it jumping out of his hand, with the net still twisted around it. But the third time he tried the fish at last slithered free, splashing and leaping in the shallows and turning all the waterdrops to tears of gold. Then the fish raised its head out of the waves and said, 'For your kindness, Prince, I can offer you three wishes. One for each attempt you made to help me. But you must think well and choose wisely, for I can only grant you one of the three.'

"Was that...?" began Tod.

"Sheesh!" breathed Mim. "Shush. The Prince thought carefully," she continued, "and then he said, 'Of course, I know. I wish for my hollow place to be filled.'

'No,' said the fish, 'for that is no longer necessary, it is almost filled already.'

So the Prince thought again and he said, 'I wish for the Mouse to live with me for the rest of my days.'

'No,' said the fish. 'For the Mouse's work is done and her ending is different from yours.'

Then the Prince, much saddened, said, 'Then I do not know. I have no other wish.' But at once the Mouse whispered in his ear and he said, with some surprise, 'I wish... I wish to go... to the House with the Green Door.'

And immediately the fish with a cry of 'Granted', disappeared into the waves and a great wind came whooshing across the pool. It lifted the Prince into the air and swept him up, up and away whirling him high among the clouds before setting him gently on the ground right in front of the House with the Green Door."

Mim's voice dwindled to a stop. Tod became aware of people moving around him, pressing towards the steps where, very close, the ferry boat was bobbing and chugging on the choppy water.

"Is that all?" he asked. "I mean... what is there... what's behind the green door?"

But Mim was silent.

Stiffly Tod stood up. The ferryman was already handing out the passengers who had come from the town on the other side and they were climbing up through those who were waiting to go over. Tod looked around searching for a kindly face, for anyone he might possibly ask for money. But there was no-one. No-one. Everyone ignored him, brushing past as though they didn't see him; as if he simply wasn't there at all. The words of the Tramp on the heath came back to him. "That's right! Turn your face from the unsightly poor... the outcast... the wanderer..." and in desperation he shuffled up to the back of the little crowd, hoping perhaps to hide among them and creep on board unnoticed. But the ferryman, looking up, spotted him there and, scowling, shouted–

"Hey you! I've told you once already! No free lifts! Clear off, will you!"

Tod dropped back. The last incoming passenger mounted the steps and the first outgoing one started to descend. Softly in his ear he heard Mim say, "Take the locket, Tod. Take the locket and give it to the ferryman."

Tod's throat felt tight and his breath came short and painfully. He shook his head. "Quick," said Mim. "Quick!" And slowly, slowly, Tod began to undo the knot on the scarf which bound her to him.

As the scarf loosened he swung her round into his arms. There were only four or five people ahead of him now and the rain was falling in solid sheets. Mim's pale face glimmered wanly up at him, but her mouth twitched and then curved into a wide, happy smile.

"Don't be sad, Tod," she said. "Go on. Take it!"

Tod's cold, wet fingers fumbled with her Mimosa jumper and found the locket heart. And even as he touched it, the pin so jammed and immoveable before, released its grip on the threadbare cloth of her suit. She let out a little trembling sigh and murmured, "Be happy... happy... happy..." before the locket dropped into his hand and with a heaving breath that seemed to split his own chest, he leapt down the steps and thrust it under the nose of the ferryman.

The man, ready to cast off, looked taken aback. The boat rocked under him as he stepped heavily to one side. He looked at the golden locket and he looked at Tod. Then his fingers closed greedily around it and with a jerk of his head he indicated an empty seat in the stern.

Tod, clutching Mim tight, his face melting into the falling water, his heart thundering like a beaten drum, staggered down the boat and dropped in to the seat Mim's heart had bought him.

Chapter 22

As the ferry boat, reeking of oil and exhaust fumes, laboured against the thrash of the rain and the thrust of the current to turn into the creek, Tod shuddered out of the numbness which had gripped him ever since he had sat down in the stern.

Rain lashed him, streaming off his hair and face, soaking through to his skin. The other passengers sat sunk in their own thoughts, shrunk into themselves under its stinging assault. Dense billows of cloud rolled down the mountain side and in their darkening shadow the boat bucked and reared, sending showers of spray to meet the falling rain. As the whole world seemed about to be overwhelmed in water, Tod at last looked down at Mim.

She lay across his knees utterly still and silent. She would never speak again, he knew that. With her heart gone her story, like that of the Mouse, had come to its natural end. Whatever mysterious place she had come from, whoever she was, she had brought him safely back to himself — to where he needed to be. And although her heart was gone and she would not speak again, he understood as clearly as if she had told him herself, that it was with her voice that *his* new heart would learn to speak. He could not imagine life without her, but he also knew that it was right, that it was time — now — for her to go.

So as the boat crossed the bar and entered the quieter waters of the creek, Tod drew the black scarf over Mim's face and then wrapping it carefully around her limp body, enfolded her entirely. The turning tide dragged at the water in the creek and the boat hesitated. In this momentary lull Tod bowed his head and slipping Mim over the side of the boat, lowered her gently into the water.

"Remember..." he whispered.

The waves rose up, reached out for her.

"I'll always, always remember," he said.

Then the water received her. Swirling around her shrouded form, it rocked her away from him and while the boat nosed strongly on, the river took Mim into itself and carried her on the retreating tide, out towards the sea.

It was a strange homecoming, Tod had no doubt that it was a homecoming for his heart felt it and his feet found their own way.

As he squelched up the street from the harbour in the creek, water streamed off him as though he were a drowned man returning from the river. But the rain had stopped and in the clear, colourless sky one star hung like a marking light low over the shoulder of the mountain.

Up and up he climbed, following the main street of the small town as it tracked to and fro across the lower slopes of the hill. Around him shops were closing, street lights coming on. There was hardly anyone about, only a few late shoppers hurrying home. Along the street, stone houses huddled shoulder to shoulder and rose in grey, white and sepia tiers, higgledy-piggledy up the hill. Here and there a cobbled alleyway or a crooked flight of steps twisted up among them, but Tod ignored all side turnings and climbed steadily on.

In his drenched clothes, lacking the accustomed warmth of Mim on his back, he was colder than he had ever been in his life. The cold ate into his flesh sending long uncontrollable shudders through him, shaking him from head to foot so that he felt at any minute he might fall apart. He was altogether alone. And more lonely than he had ever been since the day his mother died.

At last the road he was walking on emerged into open space and levelled out, running along a contour of the hill. Below him the wet rooftops of the town gleamed in the last of the daylight. Trails of smoke drifted up from its chimneys. Briefly he stopped and looked down at it. Through the gaps between the houses he could see the river glinting up at him with a dark light of its own.

Where, he wondered, was Mim now.

"Home again... home again... jiggety-jig."

The words came singing softly into his head as if from a great way off and mingled there with the sound of the sea wind and the memory of Mim's laughter.

Summoning up all the small remaining strength and courage he had, Tod staggered on.

The farther he went the more scattered the houses became. Above and between them he could see the black bulk of the mountain lit only by an occasional spark of light where a cottage or farmhouse had not yet had its curtains drawn.

Then he spotted it.

A plain, stone house, it stood well back from the road across a square of grass. There was no fence and no gate but a flagged path led over the grass to two white steps under an open porch. And within the porch the weak light of a small electric lantern exposed the colour of the door. A green door. Bright apple green. With glass panels in the top half through which he could see an even weaker light shed from somewhere deep inside the house.

Tod had no idea how long it took him to walk up the path. It seemed to take for ever before he stood at last on the steps and saw with a shock that far from it being out of reach, he was eye to eye with the brass fish door-knocker. He laid his hand on its cold yellow scales and under the force of his trembling it juddered against the door beneath.

From down in the town he heard a mellow bell strike the hour, five perhaps, or six, and within the house he could hear a piano being played. Muted by distance the notes rippled up and down a sorrowful little scale. On and on, like an unstoppable musical grieving.

Tod raised the brass fish as high as it would go and let it fall heavily, once, twice, onto the door. The piano stopped. He knocked a third time. The light in the hall brightened. Silhouetted against it, but blurred and shapeless behind the frosted glass a figure approached. There was a scuffling sound, the rattle of a lock and then the door was wrenched open.

Behind the green door stood a woman.

She was tall and slender and at first Tod took her to be young, but realised almost instantly that she was not. Her shoulders were slightly bowed as she stood, blinking out into the darkness from wide slanting green eyes which peered at him over the top of gold-rimmed spectacles.

A long black woollen skirt reached almost to her ankles and above it she wore a loose tunic of some grey silky material. Faded silvery-gold hair was piled on top of her head in an untidy bunch of curls held together there by a broad black ribbon. Straightening up she drew back slightly into the hallway before she spoke.

"Well!" she said "Now what have you forgotten?"

Shivering, shaking, scattering water drops from his hair, his flesh, his clothes, Tod stood and stared at her dumbfounded. His aching head could make no sense of her question. For although the words seemed in a way to connect directly with him, he had the feeling they were not meant for him at all. The woman sighed.

"I'm sorry," she said. "I didn't meant to be cross. But you're such a scatter-brain!"

And it was then that he knew her.

By the hidden laughter in her voice, by the lilting burr that softened its gruffness, he remembered.

He remembered!

He opened his mouth to try and utter the name that had risen now to the surface of his mind but before he could force it out through his chattering teeth she stooped forward to look more closely at him. He saw the dark smudges beneath her green eyes and then her already pale face went as white as the wall behind her. She swayed and gasped and clutched at the brass door handle.

"Tom!" she whispered, "Tom?"

And then she was back through the door and trying to close it and he was straddling the threshold and trying to keep it open until he at last expelled the word, the name he had found for her...

"Nan," he sobbed. "Don't, Nan. Nan it's me... It's Tod... I've come home..."

Her little whimpers of fear stopped and she reeled back against the wall, releasing the door so suddenly that Tod lost his balance and fell at her feet. She hauled him up and pushing her glasses back on to the bridge of her nose she gazed at him — as if she might devour him. Then she ran her fingers through his hair, traced the line of his nose, squeezed the water from the sleeve of his coat and while he squirmed and tried to wriggle free, she too began to sob. And then to laugh. And then to sob again.

"It can't be," she said. "You can"t be... give me some... give me some proof... where have you come from?... Where?... And how...? How did you find me...?"

Her babble of words strangled to a stop as Tod, suddenly exhausted, unable to move or speak or think, slumped against the green door of his grandmother's house and slid slowly down it to lie stretched on the tiles of the hall in a pool of tears and rain and river water.

Chapter 23

For weeks while the winter rain fell and it blew and froze and rained again, Tod lay ill. In the long hard months of his journey he had outgrown and outworn his strength. But slowly, as the days lengthened and the early sun shining in through his bedroom window strengthened and grew warm, he began to recover.

In the room which she told him had once been his mother's, his grandmother nursed him. Though the doctor advised it, she refused to let him go into hospital.

"I'd waited so long — given up hope," she said. "Now for a while... until he is well... I can't bear to let him out of my sight."

The doctor gave in.

The room was spacious, high and airy. Morning sunlight glancing through the branches of an apple tree outside the window dappled its walls with light. It was sparsely furnished. A chequered blue quilt covered the bed and at the open window white curtains ruffled in the breeze that breathed constantly in from the sea.

At first Nan scarcely left his side except to prepare a meal, soups and purees, jellies and custards that slid smoothly down his burning throat. In his hours of wakefulness they began, sometimes with painful difficulty, to learn how to live together after their long and different experiences of solitariness.

"I've spent so much time," said Nan, "with only my ghosts for company. It's little wonder I mistook you for one of them, Tod. But I'd forgotten how a real live, flesh and blood boy has his own... complications... and is full of surprises...!"

Later when he was beginning to recover, she would leave him now and then to go downstairs and give a piano lesson to one of her pupils.

"Until you knocked on the door," she said, "only the children and the music could banish the ghosts."

Occasionally she stayed down there in the big living-room where the piano stood and played for him herself, the strong notes ringing like muffled bells through the bedroom floor. Even more occasionally she sang.

"You know all Mim's songs," he mumbled once.

And Nan smiled.

"She used to tell me stories too," he said.

He remembered Mim's last story; how she said that sometimes the endings of stories were actually beginnings in disguise. Turning his face wearily to the wall, Tod wondered how long he would have to wait for his own story to resolve itself. Ever since he had arrived at the house with the green door it seemed to have snagged somewhere, caught between an end and a beginning.

"When you are absolutely better, Tod," said Nan, "we shall have to think about school. At midsummer you'll be twelve..."

"Sheesh!" said Tod. "I don't know anything... I've missed so much!... I couldn't..."

Gently Nan tweaked the blue coverlet out of his fingers which were twisting and creasing it into a knot. "I think... you know a great deal..." she said.

"I don't even know my name," he wailed. "Not my proper name."

"It's Thomas Edward," she reminded him. "It was your mother who concertina-ed Tom and Ted into Tod. Because she couldn't decide which to call you!"

"Thomas Edward what?" asked Tod. But fell asleep before she could answer him.

One evening he sat bolt upright out of sleep and saw her sitting under the shaded lamp, watching him, her hands curled lightly round an unopened book.

"I should have sent a card to Annabel," he cried.

"Hush," she said "I already have. I did it for you."

"What did you say? What did you tell her?"

"That you're safe — and with me," she answered, crossing

the room to settle him. "And I thanked her, of course..."

"It should have been me!" panted Tod, pushing her away. "I must get up... I must go... I can't breathe in this room..."

But gradually he came to like the quiet order of the days in his room. He felt ill less often, stayed awake for longer. He grew strong enough at last to wobble out of bed and sit in a chair under the window where he could see the grey-green slopes of the upper mountain, breathe in the fresh air; see the spread of the land as he had in his travelling days.

"All that time," he said. "I couldn't remember this house... this place... But there must have been something... the hills perhaps... The Dream Land..."

During the weeks he'd been ill he had told Nan the whole of his story. He told it in halting mixed up episodes; the making of Mim; Annabel and the Paradise Garden; his time with Mort; the part Mim played in his journey...

"I had to give her... the locket... to the ferryman," he said, when there seemed little left to tell. "I suppose it belonged to my mother. It had letters engraved inside it. 'L' I think. And 'S'."

Nan who had been sitting beside him stood up and paced about the room. She was silent for a long time. She was wearing a lavender-blue skirt he hadn't seen before. He had never seen her in anything but black or grey. At last she stopped pacing and stood at the foot of his bed.

"L for Laura," she said. "And S for Solway. Yes. Your father gave the locket to her..."

"Mort gave it to her?" said Tod.

He tried to form a picture of such a giving, but could not. Even Mort's face and voice — once always so vividly present in his head — had grown dim and indistinct.

His grandmother sat down heavily, making his bedsprings creak.

"Not Mort," she said. "Your father."

"But Mort is my father..."

"No," she said.

There was a harsh edge to her voice he'd heard only once

before — the first time she spoke to him, when she thought he was one of her pupils who'd forgotten his music.

"There are things I must tell you," she said, "But so many... and so hard... I was waiting for you to be ready..."

"I am ready," said Tod.

Nan looked at him out of her green eyes. Beneath them the dark smudges seemed to have vanished and he saw instead the flush of colour along her cheekbones.

"Yes," she said. "I think perhaps you are... But as for me... You've returned to me like a blessing... a forgiveness... and I'm afraid..."

"Don't be," said Tod.

So, over a period of days, she, like Mim, told him a story. But it was not a fairy story. It was his own story. The story he didn't know. And it was not only his, but hers also. And his mother's and his father's and his grandfather's. It was Mort's story too.

"The story of all my ghosts," she said.

Chapter 24

"Long ago," began Nan, "it seems very long ago, I married your Grandfather, and went to live with him in his house by the sea."

"Is he dead?" asked Tod.

"Hush," said Nan, "the story itself will answer all your questions."

But instead of continuing it she went away and was away for five minutes before returning with a shallow cardboard box which she placed on the bed.

"As I said," she went on then, "I married Edward Solway. He was twenty, I was eighteen. We were very poor and very happy in those days. He worked on his father's boat, 'The Daisy May', as an inshore fisherman. When I was twenty your mother was born and we called her Laura. As she grew up we became better off — fishing was a thriving industry then on this part of the coast — and eventually when his father retired, Ted took over 'The Daisy May'. He also joined the Lifeboat Service."

Nan paused and opened the cardboard box. She rummaged in it for a second or two and then produced a photograph in a tarnished silver frame. "When your mother died," she said, "I put all my photographs at the bottom of a deep dark drawer. But here's your grandfather — as he was at that time..." and she handed Tod the picture.

His grandfather's face stared up at him out of the oval frame, an open face tanned and lined by wind and weather. From under a mass of tight black curls two piercing blue eyes seemed to examine Tod with a slightly amused expression.

"Like your mother," said Nan. "And like her too he was a great teller of tales. I fell in love with him because he told such stories!" She smiled and taking the picture from Tod she stood it on his dressing table before continuing.

"Laura went to the local schools. She was averagely clever, but very artistic, and long before she was sixteen she'd decided to go to Art College. Then... on her sixteenth birthday... she met your father..."

"Thomas?" asked Tod, making a guess.

Nan touched his hand lightly. "Yes," she said, "Thomas Thursday".

Tod's fingers gripped hers in surprise. "Thursday?" he repeated.

"I know," she said, "It's an odd name — but not uncommon around here".

"No," said Tod "It's not that. It's just... just that... if Thomas Thursday was my father... I must be 'Thursday's Child'..."

"Of course," said Nan, "and Thursday's child has far to go."

"That's it," murmured Tod. "That's what Mim used to say... but I thought it was to do with being born on a Thursday..."

Nan shook her head. "You were born on a Tuesday," she said.

She took a sheet of paper from the box and smoothing it out she showed him a drawing of a boy's head. It was done in pencil and crayons, the colours so lightly applied that the face and fair hair looked almost transparent, as though the paper could not hold the image, but was gradually letting it go into air and dust.

"Your mother drew it," said Nan "soon after they met."

Tod gazed at the picture of his father. At the boy's face. At his own face. His hand trembled and he let the paper drop.

"What happened?" he asked.

Nan shook her head as if she could not go on. For minutes she sat staring out of the window at the breathing branches of the apple tree before at last she began again.

"Your grandfather had known your father since he was a child — less than your age — he was the son of another fisherman. But Laura and he went to different schools and they never met until that day — when he came with a friend to her birthday. He was seventeen — almost eighteen... And that was it! From then on school work, art work, plans for the future all went to the winds. They only wanted each other. They wanted to get married but we said no — too soon — too young — education first and then we'll see..."

"So how...?" asked Tod.

Nan put her finger to his lips and went on in a great rush, "One day — a lovely late October day it was — your father came to see us. He was clearly nervous... colour coming and going in his face... his hands first in his pockets and then fiddling with his jacket, his hair... and he told us... he told us that Laura was pregnant and that they would marry each other... come what may..."

"Me?"

"Oh, yes!" said Nan. "You are right!"

"Trouble from the very beginning!" remarked Tod.

Nan laughed but sobered quickly, returning at once to her story. "Laura was out... deliberately, I suppose... and your grandfather who was usually a mild man... and who loved Tom anyway... was furious. I'd never seen him so angry. He accused Tom... of betraying our trust... of wrecking Laura's life... and much, much worse. Tom stood his ground... but he was terribly upset... and I, to my shame, was too afraid to intervene. I went out into the garden and stayed there till the row was over..."

She was rocking slightly, her eyes closed, as if the memory were too present and too painful to bear. "At last Tom left," she said. "He took his small dinghy and went out of the bay... rowing miles out... to think and... recover... I suppose. The sea was calm... silky... innocently beautiful..."

Tod sat up, holding his breath, staring at her.

"Beautiful," she repeated. "Until a storm blew up. One of those sudden vicious tempests that come striking out of the west without warning. Tom was far, far out. He was experienced — experienced and wise enough — to have distress flares with him. But in that small boat, so far from shore, he hadn't a chance..." Her voice dropped almost to nothing. "Even... even the lifeboat hadn't a chance... Your grandfather went of course... in a dreadful state... and I suppose, because of his... his love... his guilt, he made bad judgements... went too far in search... whatever the reason, the lifeboat never returned..."

Tod thought of his father and grandfather. Who had never seen him. Who could never know him. Who might have loved and been loved by him. Who died, in part, because of him. He felt as cold, as washed out and empty, as if it were he who had spent that night in the murderous sea.

Nan, noticing his shivering, threw a blanket round his shoulders and fussed over him until he protested roughly and said, "Go on. Go on. That's not the end."

"No," she said, "though for months... for years... to Laura and me... it seemed like it... And the sea that I'd once loved... I couldn't endure the sight or sound of the sea... So we left the house where we lived and moved inland, here under the mountain. The only reminder of that other place we brought with us was the brass fish door-knocker! I've never been back to the sea since... though I hear it every time the wind blows through the trees..."

"What about... what about me?" asked Tod.

Nan came out of her reverie, brightened and smiled.

"Without you," she said, "we might never have made it. You were born in this house and we brought you up together. You looked like your father. You made us laugh — like your grandfather. You were our new beginning."

Tod thought again of Mim.

"I sent Mim... to join them," he said.

"Yes," said Nan.

"And the green door... the door with the fish knocker... I must have remembered that from when I was small..."

"Five," said Nan. "You were here until you were almost five. In the spring before your fifth birthday, things changed."

"Mort?" asked Tod.

"Yes. Mort. But I think you've had enough for one day. Before I tell you that part of the story we'll see if you're strong enough to walk out in the garden."

Chapter 25

They sat in a sheltered corner where the house wall met the garden wall. On the far side of the lawn, under the trees of Nan's small orchard, the first golden trumpets of the daffodils were beginning to show through the long grass. Out of the wind the sun was warm.

"Your mother was so young," said Nan. "She was only seventeen when you were born. There were times when I felt more like the mother of you both and she seemed more like your sister. I earned money teaching — as I do now. And she earned too — by sewing for people. It wasn't what she wanted, but she had plans for going on with her education once you were settled at school.

Then she went one night with friends to visit the Fair that comes here every Easter — and Mort was working on the rides."

"Mort worked at a Fair?" interrupted Tod, recalling with a shock the dream he'd had on the aeroplane.

Nan sniffed and plucked a weed out from a crevice in the wall.

"Oh, yes." she said. "At that time. He was handsome too in a dark, romantic, gypsy kind of way... And she'd had no boy-friend since your father... no-one... Anyway she went back to the Fair several times that week! She took you once I think... And then, when the Fair left, Mort stayed."

"Didn't you like him?"

"I detested him. But then I saw him as a threat to my security. As indeed he was... He had a voice too — smooth and dark as black treacle but with a kind of gritty edge to it — very pleasant to listen to..."

"Did he?" asked Tod. He shook his head in disbelief. "He said horrible things with it," he muttered.

"Not to her. Not then. He sweet-talked her into loving him. And then there was his past... his childhood... and she felt sorry for him. Some truly horrible things had happened to him..."

"I know he was struck twice by lightning," said Tod, "It had left white stripes across his hair."

Nan looked at him, her eyebrows kinked right up under her fringe. Then she laughed.

"What a tale!" she said. Then more soberly she added, "It was much worse than lightning, Tod. His hair went white like that when he was very young... because of the things he saw, the things that were done to him..."

Tod started to ask what had happened to Mort, but before he had said two words Nan stopped him. "That's not part of this story," she said. "And what he told your mother may or may not be true... Like the story of the lightning!... Anyway," she went on, "in spite of my opposition... perhaps because of it... he persuaded Laura to go away with him. And she, of course, would not leave you... So... so I lost you both..."

"Why?" said Tod, pained, "Why didn't you keep... keep in touch?"

"You may well ask," said Nan. Her face had darkened again and she turned it from him. "I was so angry... hurt... and then... so stubborn! I refused to write... to answer her letters... and eventually lost track altogether... until..."

"Until what?"

"Until Mort wrote to say... to say she had died."

"But I hadn't died," mumbled Tod. With a sudden flash of anger he seized her arm and pulled her roughly round to face him.

"Why didn't you come for me then?" he cried. "Why did you leave me with Mort... who was so cruel...?"

Nan winced. She reached for his hands, but he snatched them away.

"I did, Tod," she said. "I travelled the length and breadth of the country. I wrote hundreds of letters, saw dozens of people. Mort's letter about your mother came from one city but I found at last she was buried in quite another. Mort travelled constantly, always ahead of me. As fast as I picked up his trail he was up and away. No school — in any place where I found a scent — had ever heard of you. After months and months of searching I had drawn a blank. It was like trying to follow shadows, phantoms. You seemed to have disappeared into the air itself... And then... like you... I fell ill..."

Tod sank back into his chair. The sun slanted warmly across his chest where his heart was beating strong and fast. Thinking of the years with Mort he saw that his grandmother's story was true.

"He was a... he was... my... wicked stepfather," he said, with a short laugh.

"Yes," said Nan, "Though not 'stepfather' in a legal sense. He had — he has — no real claim on you at all. He and your mother, you know, were never married."

"But how could my mother love him when he was so wicked?" asked Tod. "And why was he...?"

Nan sighed.

"I don't know the answer to either of those questions," she said, "except... Mort did most certainly love her... And no-one can know, can they, I mean no-one can really know... what drives another person? The only inside story we know is our own and even at that we don't always... read... it clearly. Mort was like a wounded animal... Maybe it was that... his own suffering... which made him want to hurt and destroy..."

"I suppose," said Tod.

He scuffed his new shoes on the stones of the yard and brooded on this for a while. Above their heads the wind took hold of a last dead leaf on the stem of a climbing rose, twirling it, tapping it against the wall.

"Sometimes," he said, "I feel so angry... I have such black thoughts... I often wanted to kill Mort!"

His grandmother stayed motionless in one of her long silences before, turning to him, she said, "But everyone has feelings like that, Tod. They're part of us. Like... like the weeds in the garden. We probably can't uproot them altogether... but we can choose... we can choose not to nourish them..."

She stopped. And in the silence Tod noticed for the first time the music the birds were making — brief glittering threads of sound which they seemed to stitch into the air. He saw Nan raise her head and smile. She too was listening. Then, as if to try and banish the gloom of her words, the sadness of the story she had told him, she began to hum a little song. It was under her breath at first but as she found words to add to the tune she began to sing aloud and Tod recognized the melody as one of Mim's. He started to join in, zizzing through his teeth as she had so often done. Nan looked at him in surprise, giggled and then sang louder still.

"La-la-la-la sport today
La-la-la tomorrow
Love la-la-la-flies away
La-la-la-la-sorrow
Dance and sing
Time's on the wing
But la-la-la-the return of Spring..."

She seemed to have forgotten most of the words and as Tod tried to match his voice to hers he found it wouldn't do what he wanted. It squeaked one minute and growled the next until what with that and the nonsense she was singing, Nan began to laugh so much that her own voice cracked and the song collapsed altogether.

"It's true though, isn't it?" she said, when at last she could speak. She stood up, opening her arms to the garden. "Spring is on its way! I'd forgotten what it felt like!"

Chapter 26

Spring came in with a rush on the last day of April. Before it grew light a fanfare of birds in the garden woke Tod up from a deep sleep. He yawned, stretched, covered his head with a pillow and fell asleep again. Much later, the sunlight lapping warmly across his bed, woke him a second time. Kicking off the quilt he cycled his legs in the air to cool them before bounding out of bed. Against a shining blue sky the mountain, still in shadow, seemed close enough to leap to from the window. Clumps of yellow gorse blazed like bonfires on its upper flanks and lower down the woods had broken out in a rash of green. Golden light fizzed among the tender new leaves of the apple tree and as Tod peered down through its branches he thought, "Bet I could climb that — when I'm better." And even as he thought it, he realised that he was better, that he was at last truly well.

As he pulled on his jeans and T-shirt, still stiff and unfamiliar in their newness, he caught sight of himself in the mirror on the wall. The mirror, the only one in the house — for Nan had banished mirrors when she banished photographs — was his own, the last remnant of his treasures. The glass, in its frame of leaves and flowers, had been repaired so that now he could see his face whole, unscarred by cracks or blotches. He stared at himself. Where had this boy come from? Surely his nose and chin were bigger than they had been? Certainly his eyes were different. Large and slightly slanting like Nan's they were no longer the colour of rain but like hers too, they were green and flecked with gold around the pupil...

There was a tap on the door and he turned away from the mirror as his grandmother came in. In her hand she held a cream envelope which she placed on his dressing table. Reading it he saw it was addressed in a bold, rather scrawling hand to Tod Solway.

With a tremor of pleasure and surprise he picked it up.

"Listen," said Nan, "Listen, Tod. It's a beautiful day — and I've only one early lesson to give — and it's time you went out — time we both left the house and garden — and I've thought and thought..."

She hesitated. Tod saw that she was wearing a summer frock, ivory cotton splattered with scarlet poppies and bright blue cornflowers. He guessed she hadn't worn such a frock for years. He smiled at her and twitched his eyebrows up and down. She laughed and then rushed on, "In short", she said "I thought we would take a picnic and go... we could go to the sea..."

"Sheesh!" said Tod.

She didn't wait for any more response but whisked away and ran down the stairs as he carefully opened his letter.

"Dear Tod," he read,

"Your grandmother wrote to tell me you were much, much better. She also says you've grown into quite a bean pole which I find hard to imagine when you were such a twiglet last time I saw you. I must say the time at Drake House seems a long way off. As well as your amazing postcards (with all their detailed information — Ha!), I have had four cards from Maisie who is also much stronger, speaks Italian like a Greek (so she says) and is returning, with her father, in the summer. I hope I shall see them again soon afterwards — which brings me to the real point of this letter. In May I have an interview for a place in College in the city where your friend Robin lives — D'you remember Robin — Hey Robin! Jolly Robin! — I don't think I shall be seeing very much of him around the place — do you? Anyway, as you know, the city is not so very far from where you now live and I must say I should like to see you safe and sound and looking more like the giant than Jack! What d'you say? Your G.M. says she'd love to see me. (People often say that before they actually have) and in the end it's really up to you of course. Can you bear another encounter? If so just drop me one of your wondrous p.c.s and I'll be there!

Take care, Tramp — and don't disappear on another trek until I've seen you — all renewed, restored and polished — with my own two eyes!

Luv, Annabel."

With a laugh, Tod thrust the letter in his pocket. Downstairs he could hear someone stumbling through scales on the piano, fingers tumbling too fast over the base notes. He went down to ask Nan if he could have some money to buy one more card for Annabel...

The girl on the piano stool stopped playing when she heard his footsteps and swivelled around to look curiously at him. She was about his own age, thought Tod, with short cropped hair that was as shiny black as Mim's fur thatch had once been.

"This is Amy," said Nan formally, "and this is my grandson, Tod."

"Hello," said Amy, shyly. She fidgeted with her book of music while Tod told Nan the contents of Annabel's letter and asked about the money. Then, when he stopped speaking, Amy said, "You're starting at the High School in September aren't you?"

Tod felt momentarily cold. But he nodded and tried to smile.

"So'm I," she said.

Then as if nervous that she'd spoken out of turn she hastily folded her music and stood up.

"I'll go now, Mrs. Solway," she mumbled and with a fleeting smile at Tod, departed through the length of the room where, Tod noticed, Nan's photographs were beginning to re-appear on shelves much as the leaves were re-appearing on the trees outside.

Nan set the picnic basket on the sand and spreading an old blanket sat down and faced the sea. Along the shore a scalloped ribbon of weed decorated with shells and other sea-debris, marked the tide line. Just below it the waves advanced and retreated among swags and swirls of lacy white foam. The sea sparkled to the horizon where blue met blue in an almost invisible seam. It looked as innocent as a sheet of crumpled silk but underlying the sound of their own voices, of distant laughter, of the complaining voices of the gulls, the sea roared its steady roar.

"Before we begin our day," Nan said, "we'll exorcise our ghosts..."

"How?" asked Tod.

"Let them go... release them to the wind and the waves..."

"Like Mim," said Tod.

"Just like Mim," agreed Nan, "It's time. They know it. And I know it."

Tod sat beside her and scooping up a handful of sand let the cool grains trickle through his fingers. He thought about Mim.

"An ending... which is also a beginning?" he said.

"Yes," said Nan eagerly. "That's it exactly. A farewell and a celebration!"

She drew her knees up under her chin and clasped her arms about them.

"Thou are the Stranger I know best," she murmured.

"Is this a prayer?" he asked, startled.

She shook her head. "Listen," she said.

"Thou art the Stranger I know best
Thou art the sweet heart, who
Came from the land between Wake and Dream,
Cold with the morning dew."

Tod listened, savouring the words.

"I'm not sure I understood that," he said.

Nan smiled and drew the picnic basket towards her. "It doesn't matter," she said. "It doesn't matter at all..."

She started to unpack the basket, laying a cloth on the sand, plates on the cloth. "What matters," she said, "is that you and I have returned from the dead... And both of us perhaps... stronger... for having been there and back."

She unwrapped greaseproof paper, laid out sandwiches, prised the lid from a bowl of salad.

She was right, thought Tod. He did feel strong. He felt ready for anything. He looked about him and saw that more people were coming down on to the beach. A family, settling just behind them, opened folding chairs, set up a windbreak, brought out food and bottles of fizz.

"Can I have a sandwich?" he asked.

"*Please*," said Nan.

So Tod took one — and Nan tutted because that was not what she meant — and then took one herself.

"When I go to school," said Tod, his mind still on new beginnings, "what will you do?"

From behind them a child, rushing head down and headlong towards the sea, threatened to trip over Nan's outstretched feet. She reached out a hand to steady him.

"What I should like to do," she said, as the child went on its way, "is to tell your story... write it down..."

"Sheesh!" said Tod.

"Just for ourselves," she said. "So that... in the dark times...we'll remember."

Blinking into the dazzle of the light coming off the sea Tod found it hard to imagine the dark.

"What would you call it," he asked, "if you wrote it?"

Nan hesitated. Then she said, "When you were small, you used to love a poem called 'Someone.'"

Tod laughed. "So that's what you're going to call my story!" he said. The sun had grown very hot. Tugging his T-shirt out of his jeans he pulled it over his head. "It would be better to call it 'No-one'!" he added, his voice muffled through the cloth.

His grandmother scored lines through the sand with her bare heels.

"Certainly not!" she said, "After all — by the time you knocked on my door you were already..."

"What?" asked Tod.

"Well..." she said, "Someone!"

They both giggled. A group of children with buckets and spades had gathered near the water's edge. They began to dig and heap the sand, patting and shaping it, gouging a moat, building a wall.

"Anyway," said Nan. "It's the first line of that poem I want for the title."

Tod took an apple from the basket and stood up in a shower of sand. At the sea edge one of the children looked up and waved.

"I can't remember it," he said. "Not that one..."

He smiled down at Nan and then dropping the apple into her lap he started to move away. Nan bit into the apple.

"I shall call it," she said, "*Someone Came Knocking*."

But Tod, crossing the ribbons of sea weed, almost at the sea, did not hear.

Stripping off his shoes and socks, he asked the waving child for her bucket and wincing as the cold, bright water washed about his toes, he stooped and filled it to the brim.